TODD STRASSER

GIVE A BOY A GUN

20th ANNIVERSARY EDITION

SIMON & SCHUSTER BFYR

New York London Toronto Sydney New Delhi

An imprint of Simon & Schuster Children's Publishing Division
1230 Avenue of the Americas, New York, New York 10020

For information about special discounts for bulk purchases, please contact Simon & Schuster Special Sales at 1-866-506-1949 or business@simonandschuster.com.
The Simon & Schuster Speakers Bureau can bring authors to your live event. For more information or to book an event, contact the Simon & Schuster Speakers Bureau at 1-866-248-3049 or visit our website at www.simonspeakers.com.
Also available in a SIMON & SCHUSTER BFYR hardcover edition
Book design by Krista Vossen
The text for this book was set in Adobe Caslon Pro.
Manufactured in the United States of America
This SIMON & SCHUSTER BFYR paperback edition May 2020
2 4 6 8 10 9 7 5 3 1
The Library of Congress has cataloged the hardcover edition as follows:
Strasser, Todd.
Give a boy a gun / Todd Strasser.
1st ed.
146 p. ; 22 cm.
Summary: Events leading up to a night of terror at a high school dance are told from the point of view of various people involved.
Notes: Includes bibliographical references (pp. 144-146).
ISBN 978-978-1-5344-6450-6 (hc) • ISBN 978-978-1-5344-6461-2 (pbk)
ISBN 978-1-4391-1521-3 (eBook)
[1. School shootings—Fiction. 2. High schools—Fiction. 3. Schools—Fiction.] Title.
PZ7.S899 Gir 2000
[Fic] 21
2001276544

To ending youth violence.

For every young person who has ever been killed or wounded by a gun.

Acknowledgments

My sincerest thanks to my editor, David Gale, and his assistant, John Rudolph, for their insight and encouragement; and to everyone else at Simon & Schuster for giving me the opportunity to write this book; to Joanna Lewis Cole for her inspiration, suggestions, and guidance; to Jann Wenner and *Rolling Stone*, and Tom Diaz, for their dedication to fighting youth gun violence and for their generosity; to Dr. Barry Brenner of the Brooklyn Hospital/Cornell University Department of Emergency Medicine for his helpful information; to Sophie Ryan for her diligent research assistance; to Erica Stahler for her excellent copyediting; and to my family and friends for their constant interest and support.

Author's Note

One of the things I used to like about writing books for young people was that it wasn't necessary to deal with murder, adultery, and various other immoral or criminal activities that seem mandatory in adult novels these days. I find it sad and frightening that this is no longer the case.

One of the things I dislike most about guns in our society is that, like violence and sex in the media, they rob children of what we used to think of as a childhood.

The story you are about to read is a work of fiction. Nothing—and everything—about it is real.

—Todd Strasser's original author's note
Give a Boy a Gun
September 1, 2000

2020

When I wrote this book more than twenty years ago, I could not have imagined that the state of gun violence in this country would only grow significantly worse during the decades that followed. Like many other gun-control advocates, I was saddened and disappointed in 2004 when the US Congress allowed the federal ban on semiautomatic assault rifles and high-capacity magazines to expire.

Such weapons would later be used in the two deadliest

mass shootings in the history of our country—in 2016 when Omar Mateen killed 49 and wounded 53 in the Pulse nightclub in Orlando, Florida; and in 2017 when Stephen Paddock killed 58 and injured 527 by firing on concertgoers in Las Vegas, Nevada.

I also find it deeply disheartening that there are currently thirty-one states that allow the open carrying of a handgun *without a firearm license or a permit.*

And I suspect that I am not alone in finding it equally disturbing that for students in schools today, fear of active shooters lingers constantly in the backs of their minds. This fear is propelled to the forefront each time students practice a lockdown drill, pass through increased security, hear talk of teachers being encouraged to carry firearms, or are themselves instructed to report any student who threatens to commit a shooting.

This is a generation that has never known life without the possibility of being gunned down at any time or in any place. Today such violence occurs on a nearly weekly basis, and has spread outside schools to movie theaters, bars, dance clubs, and outdoor concerts. Since *Give a Boy a Gun* was originally published in 2000, the number of gun deaths in this country has risen to more than one hundred a day. To quote US Senator Robert Casey Jr. of Pennsylvania, "While the opponents of gun control continue to maintain that their right to own and carry guns is guaranteed by the Constitution, it is impossible to believe that this daily butchery of innocent children and other human beings was what the authors of the Bill of

Rights intended or expected when they wrote the Second Amendment two hundred thirty years ago."

As has been repeatedly reported in the media, hate crimes involving gun violence are on the rise. According to the National Crime Victimization Survey (NCVS), there are approximately 250,000 hate crimes committed in the US every year, targeting victims based on their actual or perceived race or ethnicity, gender or gender identity, sexual orientation, disability, or religion. Guns are a frequent tool in hate-motivated violence and intimidation. Data from the NCVS shows that from 2010 through 2016, there were 56,130 hate crimes committed in the US involving the use of a firearm.

While these are daunting and troubling developments for anyone who wishes to live in a world free from the fear of being randomly gunned down, there have been some profoundly positive advances in the battle against mass shootings, and advances for gun control as well. Since the early 2000s—when other observers and I began to link some school shootings to bullying—schools everywhere have embraced rigorous anti-bullying programs. These programs appear to have played a marked role in decreasing the number of school shooting incidents in which bullying was considered a motivating factor.

Also, the number of organizations and action committees pledging to fight for gun control has increased significantly. In the wake of tragic and devastating school shootings such as the murder of 20 six- and seven-year-olds and 6 adults at Sandy Hook Elementary School in Newton, Connecticut, and of 14 students and 3 staff members at Marjory Stoneman Douglas High School in Parkland, Florida, young people have begun taking an active role in demanding and fighting for their own protection. In addition to organizing massive protest marches and registering thousands of new voters, youth-run organizations such as March for Our Lives have helped push dozens of new gun-safety laws through state legislatures.

In 2018, after the mass shooting in Parkland, state legislatures passed sixty-nine gun-control measures—more than in any other year since the Newtown, Connecticut, massacre in 2012, and more than three times the number passed in 2017. At the same time, state legislatures rejected about 90 percent of state-level bills backed by the National Rifle Association (NRA). Concerned young people have made inroads in convincing corporate America to cut ties with the NRA and take additional steps to diminish gun violence. As a result, Dick's Sporting Goods, one of the largest sellers of guns, announced it would no longer carry military-style assault rifles and that it would not sell firearms to anyone under twenty-one.

Since the year 2000, more than six hundred thousand Americans have been killed by guns, and more than twice that number have been injured. According to the *New England Journal of Medicine*, gun violence is the second leading cause of death among children and teenagers, after car accidents. Americans are twenty-five times more likely to die from a gunshot than residents of France, Canada, Germany, and Australia. In 2018 in Japan—a country with very strict gun laws—only three people died from gun violence. In 2017 in the United States, 39,773 people died in shootings of all kinds. In the year 2000 the cost of the consequences of gun violence in our country was estimated at $100 billion. Today the cost is said to be approaching $230 billion a year.

Finally, as must be sadly obvious to anyone who follows issues regarding firearms and mass shootings, advances in gun control still seem to come only after the most horrible acts of murder. Too often when the initial outrage fades, the impetus to fight for real change also fades. Americans have by now become so used to capricious gun carnage that unless the number of deaths in a shooting reaches the double digits, people often shrug, shake their heads, and soon forget. The question that citizens of this country must ask themselves is: How many more increasingly heinous and devastating incidents involving the murder of the young and the innocent will have to occur before real steps are taken to end gun violence? Or are we all destined to spend the rest of our lives watching such acts continue in perpetuity?

"The hallways erupted in screaming, terror-stricken pandemonium as students realized this was . . . another, increasingly familiar scene: a student with a gun."

—*USA TODAY*, 5/21/99

PART OF GARY SEARLE'S SUICIDE NOTE

Dear Mom,

By the time you read this, I'll be gone. I just want you to know that there's nothing you could have done to stop this. I know you always tried your best for me, and if anyone doubts you, just show them this letter.

I don't know if I can really explain why I did this. I guess it's because I know that I'll never be happy. I know that every day of my life will hurt and be a lot more bad than good. It's entirely a matter of, What's the point of living?

Introduction

Around 10 p.m. on Friday, February 27, Gary Searle died in the gymnasium at Middletown High School. After the bullet smashed through the left side of his skull and tore into his brain, he probably lived for ten to fifteen seconds.

The brain is a fragile organ suspended in a liquid environment. Not only does a bullet destroy whatever brain tissue is in its path, but the shock waves from the impact severely jar the entire organ, ripping apart millions of delicate structures and connections. In the seconds that follow, the brain swells with blood and other fluids. The parts of the brain that control breathing and heartbeat stop. One doctor described it to me as "an earthquake in the head."

At the moment of Gary's death I was in the library at the state university, where I was a sophomore studying journalism. As soon as I heard the news, I went home to Middletown, determined not to leave until I understood what had happened there.

Returning to Middletown was like stepping into a thick fog of bewilderment, fury, agony, and despair. For weeks I staggered through it, searching out other lost, wandering souls. Some were willing to talk to me. Others spoke because they felt a need to defend themselves even though no one had pointed an accusing finger at them. Some even sought me out because they *wanted* to talk. As if speaking about it was a way of trying to figure it out, of beginning the long, painful process of grieving and moving ahead.

Some refused to speak because it must have been too painful. For others, I suspect it was because they had learned something about themselves that they were still struggling to accept—or to conceal.

I spoke to everyone who would speak to me. In addition I studied everything I could find on the many similar incidents that have occurred in other schools around our country in the past thirty years.

The story you are about to read is really two stories. One is about what happened here in Middletown. The other is the broader tale of what is happening all around our country—in a world of schools and guns and violence that has forever changed the place I once called home. The quotes and facts from other incidents are in a different-style print. What happened in Middletown is in plain print.

This, then, is the story of what I learned. It is told in many voices, in words far more eloquent and raw than any I could have thought of on my own. It is a story of heartbreak and fear and regret. But mostly it is a warning. Violence comes in many forms—guns, fists, and words of hate and contempt. Unless we change the way we treat others in school and out, there will only be more—and more horrible—tragedies.

—Denise Shipley

About Gary

Mrs. Searle and Gary moved into the house next to ours the day before second grade began. So the first time I actually saw him was at the bus stop. He was kind of quiet, but friendly enough. Some of the kids at the bus stop would play soccer in the street in the morning. I was glad when Gary came along, because I wasn't into that, and with Gary there it gave me something to do. We'd mostly talk about stuff like Magic cards and video games and what we saw on TV.

If you want to know the truth, I think Mrs. Searle was a little overprotective. I guess because she was the only parent. She always wanted to know where Gary was going, and would he be warm enough, and junk like that. Gary would just roll his eyes.

Until Brendan came along, I think I was pretty much Gary's best friend. The thing about Gary was that mysterious part of him that you never knew. It was like something he kept hidden and private. I can't explain it, but I could feel it when I was with him. He'd just get quiet and you knew he was a billion miles away. I

In the United States in 2018, guns killed an average of 100 people a day and injured an additional 300.

always thought maybe it was something about his parents getting divorced.

—Ryan Clancy, a friend of both
Gary's and Brendan's

Gary Searle was a very sweet little boy with slightly red-dish brown hair and big, round eyes. He was polite and quiet and always did what he was told. I do recall that some of the children teased him about his weight. But you know how kids are at that age.

—Ruth Hollington, Gary's fourth-grade teacher
at Middletown Elementary School

I didn't move to Middletown until fifth grade, so I didn't know Gary before that. After we started hanging out, he'd sometimes talk about what it was like when he was younger. About the divorce and how completely nasty it was, and how after it was over, his dad just left and never paid child support or called or anything. That was a huge thorn in Gary's side. He just couldn't get over that.

—Allison Findley, Gary's on-and-off girlfriend
at Middletown High School

"As parents, teachers, and other adults look for ways to reach out to young people, some see a common thread in the disappointments and isolation students experience when they lose a sense of place, lose a parental figure, or lose a girlfriend."

—*Christian Science Monitor***, 5/26/99**

It was an ugly divorce. All that yelling and fighting. Arguing over money. Gary was caught in the middle, and sometimes I guess I used him to get what I thought I needed. What we both needed. It's a terrible thing to put a child through, but I didn't know what else to do.

—Cynthia Searle, Gary's mother

Gary was enormously bright. You wouldn't know it, because he was one of the quiet ones; never raised his hand. I noticed it first in math. He almost always did perfectly on his quizzes, unless he made a careless mistake. But the computer was the real tip-off. I wanted to do a class Web page. Gary volunteered to do it. No matter what the problem, he seemed to know three ways to fix it.

—Stuart McEvoy, Gary's sixth-grade teacher at Middletown Middle School

A lot of kids play computer games and junk, but it was different with Gary. The thing about him was he was on [the computer] all the time. I'd call his house and he'd answer with this faraway voice, and I'd know he was online. He'd sound weird because there'd be this split-second delay in his conversation, and those typing sounds. Like he was doing two things at once. Then one day I was over there, looking over his shoulder. He had three instant message screens open and was chatting with someone different in each one. *And* he was on the phone. That's when I realized that when I called, he wasn't doing two things at once. He was doing four.

—Ryan Clancy

I brought [Gary] to a psychologist. I hoped he'd let out a little of what he was feeling. She said he was guarded. I don't think she ever got close to what was going on in his head. It's obvious now that none of us did.

—Cynthia Searle

I'll give you an example of how bright Gary was. After the first month of sixth grade I got a message one day to call his mother at work. I remember the phone call because she seemed reluctant to say exactly what was on her mind, but I finally got the impression that she was wondering why I didn't give more homework. Apparently, Gary rarely spent more than half an hour a night doing it. The funny thing was half the parents in the class were complaining that I gave the kids too much homework.

—Stuart McEvoy

It's easy to look back now and dissect the stuff you did for every little clue. Like one summer Gary and I had these magnifying glasses, and we'd burn bugs and caterpillars alive. It was kind of cool to watch them twist and

"The outcasts, obsessed with violent video games and intrigued by German rock music and Nazi culture, also had pastimes as wholesome as baseball; they were part of a tight circle of friends, earned top grades, held jobs and looked forward to life after graduation—factors that no doubt reassured their parents."

—*New York Times, 6/29/99*

squirm. Is that a clue? Or something a billion other kids do too?

—Ryan Clancy

I still find it difficult to believe he was part of what happened. The guns and holding those poor children hostage in the gym like that. What they did to that football player. That wasn't the Gary I knew. If you're looking for answers, don't look at him. Look at Brendan Lawlor.

—Ruth Hollington

PART OF BRENDAN LAWLOR'S SUICIDE NOTE

To the good people of Middletown:

I hope this gets printed in big, bold letters on the front page of the newspaper, because it's something every single one of you should read. I'm gone now, and you want to know why I took your kids with me?

Here's why. You made my friggin' life miserable. How? By the way you raised your kids to all want to be the same and to hate anyone who dares to be a little different. Oh, no, you're probably thinking, you didn't do that.

You sure did. I've seen you in your cars staring at me and my friends. *Look at those creeps. Look at their clothes and the music they listen to. Why can't they go out for sports or at least root for our team?*

About Brendan

Brendan Lawlor and his family lived here [in Springfield] until the middle of seventh grade [when they moved to Middletown]. I'd say from second grade on I was about his best friend. There were times when we got into fights and wouldn't talk for a while, but mostly we were friends. I always thought Brendan was a really cool kid. Popular, too.

He was smart and funny and a pretty good athlete for an average-size, thin kid. He was fast. He could really dis anyone to pieces, and he was one of those guys who would think up a cut-down right on the spot. I'll never forget one time when we were goofing on this one kid because he had B.O., and Brendan said, "Your armpits smell so bad, the teacher gave you an A for *not* raising your hand." That really cracked us up.

—Brett Betzig,
a friend of Brendan's from Springfield

Brendan was one of the more vocal boys in the class, but also a very good student. He always had his homework and projects in on time. He was very good at expressing himself on paper, although his grammar and spelling were atrocious, which is often the case with boys his age. He could be temperamental, but that's also not unusual.

—Katherine Sullivan, Brendan's sixth-grade teacher
at Springfield Middle School

You couldn't have asked for better neighbors than the Lawlors. Tom and Samantha Lawlor were so nice, always offering to help pick up a child or drive someone somewhere. They kept a neat house and a neat lawn, and I can count on one hand the number of times I heard either of them raise their voice to Brendan. I was very sorry when they moved away.

—Kit Conner, a neighbor
of the Lawlors' in Springfield

Brendan and I were on the same soccer teams because our dads were friends and they coached together. I was usually in a forward spot because I liked to score. Brendan was usually on defense. He was funny about soccer. Sometimes he'd race across the field and throw his body in front of the ball like his life depended on it, and other times he acted like he couldn't care less. I always had the feeling his dad wished he'd play harder and take it more seriously.

—Brett Betzig

"'[Mr. and Mrs. Kinkel] were devoted parents in a tight-knit family. . . . Bill had tried everything with Kip.'"
—a friend of the Kinkels', *New York Times*, 6/14/98

You know how some people seem really relaxed and at ease with themselves? Not Brendan. He never seemed comfortable. He was always a little on edge, a little wary. It was like his brain couldn't stop, even when we were just having a good time.

—Julie Shore, a friend of Brendan's
from Springfield

One thing about Brendan: He hated injustice. I remember there was this soccer game, and some kid on the other team should have been called for hands. It was really flagrant, but the ref didn't see it. A couple of seconds later their team scored. Brendan went ballistic. He was right in the ref's face, shouting and cursing like a madman. The rest of us were actually embarrassed. Mr. Lawlor had to come out on the field and take Brendan away. But Brendan just hated stuff like that.

—Brett Betzig

I was out in the front of the house when Samantha [Lawlor] drove into her driveway and got out of the car. She used to drive Brendan to school. This particular morning she looked like a wreck. Like she was going to cry. I asked if everything was okay, and she said Brendan had given her a particularly hard time that morning. I

"'Sue [Klebold] was more patient and gentle and kind with her kids than I was able to be.'"
—a friend of the Klebolds', New York Times, 6/29/99

invited her in for coffee. I think she was hoping that because I'd raised two sons, I could give her some advice.

She actually cried a little and confided in me that Brendan could be very difficult. He wasn't cooperative about doing chores, and he would blow up when he got upset. She said there were days when it was practically impossible to get him out of bed and dressed for school. It seemed so odd to me. His parents were both the opposite—even-tempered. Samantha especially was soft-spoken and gentle. Maybe he was too much for her.

—Kit Conner

We used to play video games a lot. One of our favorites was *Need for Speed*. The idea was to win the race, but we had just as much fun crashing into each other and trying to run each other off the course. Then Brendan got a demo of one of the *Doom* games. I remember we were totally blown away by it. For a couple of weeks it was all we did after school. And it was only a demo. I remember Mrs. Lawlor coming into his room one afternoon and wanting him to turn off the game and go out and play. And it was like Brendan didn't even hear her, he was so into that game. She said it again, and

---

Though violent movies, music, and video games are popular in many countries, few allow their citizens to own handguns. In 1996 handguns killed 15 people in Japan. By 2017 that number had dropped to 3 people. In the United Kingdom 30 people died from handguns in 1996. In 2017 the number was approximately 50. In Canada, it was 106 in 1996 and 130 in 2017. In the United States, 9,390 died from handguns in 1996. In 2017 that number was more than 20,000.

Brendan told her to go away. He didn't even look up. Mrs. Lawlor looked totally stunned that he'd said that. Of course, Brendan didn't notice a thing. He was too busy playing. But that was the only time I ever heard him be fresh to her.

—Brett Betzig

The day [Brendan] found out he was moving he just looked terrible. I mean, at school he looked all pale and hollow and bent. I almost thought someone in his family had died. He really didn't want to go.

—Julie Shore

The Lawlors were private people. Except for that one time with Samantha in my kitchen, she hardly ever said anything about [Brendan]. I'm not saying that's good or bad, but you had the feeling that if something was wrong, they preferred to deal with it alone and not tell the whole neighborhood. Not that I ever had a reason to believe anything was wrong, other than what I already told you. But I do know that Brendan was very unhappy about moving. That's a hard age to leave your friends.

—Kit Conner

During the first half of the twentieth century the army trained soldiers to shoot at targets with bull's-eyes. The targets were changed to human forms after it was discovered that soldiers sometimes couldn't shoot back in war even if their lives were threatened. Military psychologists have noted that video games mimic military training designed to break down the inhibition against shooting human beings.

Seventh Grade

Brendan seemed kind of lost when he first moved [to Middletown]. It was the middle of the school year, and here comes this minivan packed to the roof, and about an hour later the moving truck shows up. The moving guys started bringing furniture into the house, and the family was kind of going back and forth too. It must have been a weekend, because I went somewhere with one of my friends and his mom. I remember leaving my house and seeing Brendan out in front of his house. He just stared at me. No hello. No wave. No nothing. I think I kind of nodded at him and then got into the car and left.

A little later I come back. I'm getting out of the car, and Brendan comes out of the house and heads straight toward me carrying three tennis balls. So we start to talk, and he's asking me what school I go to and what grade I'm in and did I like this [video] game and that. You know, kind of feeling me out. And all the while he's juggling these tennis balls. It struck me as a little bizarre.

—Dustin Williams, a neighbor
of Brendan's in Middletown

I don't think he said a thing for the first two weeks. The only reason I even noticed him was because I sat in the back and

he was back there with me in science and English. The way
he looked, it was, like, wide-eyed—like a rain-forest dweller
dropped into the middle of New York City. I bet
three-quarters of the class didn't even know he was there.

—Ryan Clancy

We started talking in the hall. I mean, I was hyperaware
of him because he was new and I was new, and your
antenna is up for things like that. Like feeling all alone
and trying to connect with someone you have something
in common with, no matter what. It's like your boat just
sank and you're in the water grabbing desperately for
anything that floats.

—Emily Kirsch,
a former friend of Brendan's

I've always made a special effort with those [students] I
sense are in distress. Believe me, no one comes into this
school in the middle of the year without a lot of distress.
After the first day of class I took [Brendan] aside and told
him I knew it would be hard to adjust and that he should
take his time and not worry too much. And I remember
the way he looked at me. As if I'd caught him completely
by surprise. He may have even blinked back tears.

—Julia Reingold,
a teacher of Brendan's at Middletown Middle School

Here's this cute boy who didn't say a word for the first
three weeks, but once he started talking, it could be hard

to shut him up. At first all he could talk about was how big the school was and how much he missed all his old friends and his old school. I mean, I didn't mind it so much, because I felt like I was about the only person he had to talk to, and, frankly, I was in the same boat. But after a while it did start to get kind of repetitious, and I told him so. It was like day and night. After that, he never said a thing about his old friends or his old school.

—Emily Kirsch

According to the *New England Journal of Medicine*, gun violence is the second leading cause of death among children after car crashes.

Eighth Grade

I tried to think back to what it was like in eighth grade. It was different. I mean, it got really cliquey. But I think Brendan and I felt like, "That's okay, we're new here. They just have to get to know us." But it didn't work that way. They got to know us, but nothing changed. Instead, this whole jock and cheerleader and designer name thing just got stronger and stronger. They were like the Sun, and the rest of us were all these little planets stuck in orbits around them. After a while I think a lot of us didn't even want to be in that [popular] crowd. All we wanted was to be left alone.

—Emily Kirsch

Things in school definitely changed in eighth grade. At least for us guys on the team. Maybe it was because we knew we'd be in the high school next year. Maybe it was that some of the guys were starting to get bigger. Sometimes Coach Bosco would come over [from the high school] and watch us. You know, like he was scouting us for next year. It made us feel important. All of a sudden we were aware that we were at the brink of a bigger world. Of course, it was just high school. But to eighth graders that was a big deal.

—Dustin Williams

I don't think Brendan and Gary really clicked until around the middle of eighth grade, but once they did, it was like a lock. When I was hanging with them, I was definitely the third wheel. They were okay about it, but it was pretty obvious that I was just a visitor to whatever part of their private world they wanted me to see.

—Ryan Clancy

"Dylan Bennet Klebold grew up in a house without guns, even toy guns.

"'Tom [Dylan's father] was adamant,' said . . . a former neighbor. . . . '[He said,] "We don't need guns in the house; we're not going to play with them."'"

—*New York Times*, 6/29/99

PART OF GARY'S
SUICIDE NOTE

I could have just gone and offed myself quietly, but that would have been an even bigger waste. If I go this way, taking the people who made my life miserable with me, then maybe it will send a message. Maybe something will change, and some other miserable kid like me somewhere will get treated better and maybe find a reason to live.

In 2016 a record 27 million guns were sold in the US, 4 million more than in the previous year. This number does not include private transactions, or guns given away.

More of Eighth Grade

I thought I knew Gary better. We sort of went together on and off for nearly two years. It's obvious now that I didn't know him. Not really. I knew he had that whole other thing with Brendan. Sometimes it almost felt like they had their own language. They each just seemed to know what the other was thinking. But now it's obvious he hid a lot. Not just from me, but from everyone except Brendan.

—Allison Findley

Until Gary came into the picture, I think I was Brendan's closest friend. I can't say I was really sorry when that changed. By then I'd gotten to know some other girls who were like me—quote, unquote "outcasts"—and we were trying to have a life in spite of all that cliquey weirdness at school. I don't know why, but Brendan couldn't get past the weirdness. He was more fixated on it. It was almost all he would talk about. I was trying to get away from it. He just wanted to keep looking at it under a microscope.

—Emily Kirsch

Gary and I got into my mom's car one day. It was parked in the driveway, facing the garage. Gary sat behind the wheel, and I was next to him. He put his arm around my shoulder, and we just pretended we were driving some-where. We were staring at the garage door with big flakes of white paint peeling off it, but in our minds we were going through the desert. Gary had done that once, so he was talking about cactus and sun-bleached bones and jackrabbits and hot sun.

I leaned my head on his shoulder, and I could see it all in my mind. The two of us, all alone, driving through the desert, a million miles away from everything. Just sage-brush and creosote bushes and burned reddish cliffs. A trail of dust flying up behind us. Gary pulled me close and kissed my hair, and it was one of those really happy moments. I guess it was about as close as we ever got to blissful puppy love. Ha, ha!

Then Gary stopped. I looked up and saw that he was staring into the rearview mirror. I turned around, and Deirdre Bunson and Sam Flach and a bunch of other kids were in the street, pointing at us and laughing.

I wanted to die. Gary did too. He couldn't even turn around. He just slumped down in the seat and stared at that stupid garage door and the peeling paint. It was like they'd just stuck a knife in his heart.

Sometimes Gary and I could escape into that world where no one bothered us or laughed or made fun. But it never lasted long, and then it was like waking up from a dream and facing the cold, bald truth that it wasn't real and never would be. For the popular kids the dream was real. They lived it. They never had to be afraid of waking up.
　　　　　　　　　　　　　　　　　　—Allison Findley

Ninth Grade

It started to change at the beginning of ninth grade. I went away with my parents for two weeks in August, and Brendan and Gary stayed home and just hung with each other. When I got back, it was different. I can't exactly explain how, but I felt it. There was something dark in Brendan. I don't know where it came from. Whether it had always been inside him, or whether it just started to grow because of the way people treated him in school.

—Allison Findley

Gary wasn't always like that. When we were in eighth grade and some big jock would body-slam us into a chalkboard or rip the pocket off our shirt, we'd be pissed, and we'd grumble about how we'd like to kill this guy and kick his face in. The thing was it was all sort of make-believe wishful thinking. Maybe you'd go home and play *Doom* for an hour and just blow everyone to bits. But you

---

"The . . . cliques that rule American high schools are every bit as murderous as Harris and Klebold, only their damage is done in slow motion, over a period of many years, and fails to draw the attention of parents or teachers."

—a posting on the Internet

never *really* considered getting a gun and going after them. At least, I didn't.

—Ryan Clancy

Gary would try to play it down, make fun of it. He'd say, "Hey, doesn't matter, I'm just a loser." I'd tell him no, he wasn't a loser. But it was like he couldn't hear me. The rest of the school said he was a loser, and that just drowned me out.

—Allison Findley

People talk like our school is this sick, depraved place. That's so wrong. I talked to my mom and her friends about it, and they say it was just like this when they went to school. It must be like this at every other high school. Yes, kids can be really mean to one another, really cruel. But that's the way it's always been. I mean, isn't part of growing up just learning to deal with it?

—Deirdre Bunson

Brendan and Gary got picked on. That's a fact. We all did. Little guys; fat guys; skinny, gangly, zit-riddled guys like me. Anyone who wasn't big and strong and on a team got

---

"'Every day being teased and picked on, pushed up against lockers—just the general feeling of fear in the school. And you either respond to a fear by having fear, or you take action and have hate.'"
—Brooks Brown, a student at Columbine High who knew both Eric Harris and Dylan Klebold, *Rolling Stone*, 6/10/99

it. You'd even see big guys on the football team push around some of the smaller players. Middletown High is big and crowded, and you've got ten billion kids in the hall at once. Maybe if it's an all-out, knock-down-drag-out fight, some teacher will notice and try to stop it. But if it's just some big jerk shoving you into a locker, who's gonna see?

—Ryan Clancy

Julia [Reingold, one of Brendan's seventh-grade teachers] is a close friend and has amazing radar for the kids who are going to need support but might otherwise fall through the cracks. One of the kids she mentioned was Brendan, so I made sure he was one of mine. I got him into my office one day, and he just about "yes, ma'amed" and "no, ma'amed" me to death. "Yes, ma'am, everything's fine." "No, ma'am, I don't have a problem with anyone." But you could see the pain and anger in his eyes. Of course, I had fifty boys and girls like that, all of them feeling more or less the same thing. And I was responsible for another 350, so what could I do?

—Beth Bender,
Middletown High School counselor

Brendan was starting to get known as someone who refused to toe the line. He wouldn't bow down to the

---

Several news organizations pointed out that the ratio of students to counselors at Kipland Kinkel's high school was roughly 700 to 1.

football players. It was the fall, so in gym we were playing flag football. Usually we just went outside and messed around. There'd be two games: the "winner-athlete" game and the "loser-geek" game. That day Herr Bosco decided to show us losers the "right" way to cover a pass receiver. The thing is we were only playing flag football, just a bunch of dorks in T-shirts and shorts.

Bosco picked Sam Flach and Brendan to demonstrate. Now, you knew right away that this was no accident. Bosco hated Brendan's "attitude." So he said, "Sam and Lawlor, front and center." Jocks have first names. The rest of us mutants are last name only.

So I figure, maybe Sam's built like a brick outhouse, but Brendan's thin and fast, and I bet he'll try to beat him off the line and get free. Like, welcome to Ryan's private little football fantasy, folks. Our big chance to surprise the jocks and show them that geeks can play in the big time.

Brendan sets up on the imaginary line of scrimmage, and Sam's facing him five yards away with this smirk on his face. Like, *Come on, loser, show me what you've got.* And I'm dumb enough to be rooting for Brendan. Like, *This ain't the hall, Flach. There's room to move.*

Herr Bosco's the QB, and he yells, "Go!" Brendan takes

"Like most students, I lived in fear of the small slights and public humiliations used to reinforce the rigid high school caste system: Poor girls were sluts, soft boys were fags. And at each of my schools, there were students who lived in daily fear of physical violence."

—a posting on the Internet after Columbine

three steps, fakes left, goes right, and *POW!* Sam knocks him right on his butt. You could see Brendan didn't know what hit him. He was flat on his back, probably seeing stars.

I look around, and all the jocks are sniggering and chuckling. And the biggest smirk is on Herr Bosco's face. "Uh, Sam," he goes, "this is flag football. No hitting."

Sam just smiles back. "Gee, sorry, Coach."

You could see that Brendan was still woozy as he got to his feet. You think Bosco bothers to ask if he's okay? No, he's too busy looking for the next victim. By then I'd backed away to the rear of the crowd, where all the geeks were cowering in fear, praying Herr Bosco wouldn't pick them next.

—Ryan Clancy

Sam Flach will die slowly. I will shoot him in one knee, then the other, then a gut shot so he'll have no friggin' doubt where he's going. And he will stare up at me with a fear in his eyes he has never known, and I will put that friggin' barrel right against his forehead and say, "Gee, sorry, Sam," then blow his friggin' brains out.

—an e-mail from Brendan to Gary

To be on the outside and watch it was amazing. Except the real word for it is probably more like *horrifying*. At the red-hot core were most of the football players and some of the guys from the other teams, and the cheerleaders and some of the pretty girls. Ninety percent blondes, in case you haven't noticed.

Next came the rest of the athletes and a few popular designer label guys who weren't athletes but were just really nice and likable, and the nicer girls and some of the pretty girls who were also popular and athletic. And then came the rest of us, only it didn't matter who or what we were. And that wasn't only the way we outsiders saw it. It was the way everyone saw it. I mean, the teachers and the administrators. You'd get to class late, and they'd make you go back and get a pass. But Sam Flach would stroll in late and say he'd been talking to Coach Bosco, and that was just fine. Even the grown-ups outside school, like the guy who pumped gas at the station and the lady who worked behind the counter at Starbucks. They all knew the football players by name, and they'd do extra things for them, like wash their windshield or slip them a free brownie. There were days when you just felt like it was their world. And somehow you hadn't been picked to be part of it.

—Emily Kirsch

Everyone around here knows the football players. Either they see them at the games or they read about them in the newspaper. From about the middle of August until the end of November the sports section is all about the [Middletown] Marauders. And there'll be those human-interest stories in the other parts of the paper too. Like how Dustin Williams went to the elementary school to talk to the kids, or how Bosco got the team to spend a couple of hours cleaning up some park so kids could play there.

And there are always pictures of them, of course.

There's basketball and wrestling, too. Except the basketball team's not so hot, and even though the wrestling team is pretty good, the only people who come watch them are the wrestlers' families and friends. The baseball team is like a joke, and you never even hear about the tennis and soccer teams. Then they cover stuff like girls' field hockey and volleyball just to be politically correct.

It's like, big stories and lots of photos about football, small stories and a few photos about basketball and wrestling, and the rest is just box scores. You have to feel bad for the guys on the other teams. Unless they're total all-American superstars, they're not even noticed. And as far as the rest of us are concerned, the people in this town don't even know we exist.

—Ryan Clancy

Why shouldn't athletes be treated with more respect? They're the ones who are actually out there fighting for our school. Everybody thinks it's so great, but how do you think it feels when they lose? Each one of those players has to feel responsible for that. Everyone else walks around saying, "Oh, we would have won if so-and-so hadn't dropped the ball." Meanwhile so-and-so has to come to school, and you think he doesn't know what

---

"Outcasts loathed Columbine. With equal venom, they detested popular kids and an administration that in their minds kowtowed to the popular kids."
—*Rolling Stone*, 6/10/99

they're saying behind his back? How do you think that feels? I mean, being blamed. If [the athletes] have to take the blame for when they lose, shouldn't they get the rewards when they win? That's what school spirit is all about. The fans aren't the ones who give our school its pride. It's the players. They're the ones that give Middletown a sense of accomplishment.

—Deirdre Bunson

I love football. It's been a part of my life ever since I was small. My parents have had season tickets for the Marauders for nearly forty years. I can count on one hand the number of Friday nights we've missed. Football is part of the social fabric of this town. It brings us together and gives us something to look forward to and talk about. I firmly believe that it has a positive and long-lasting benefit for the kids, and the adults as well.

I love the excitement and the crowd and the food. I love cheering for my students and the sons of my friends. If a former student comes back to visit, I'm more likely to see him or her at the game on Friday night than anywhere else. I will be delighted if someday my own son plays for the Marauders.

You cannot blame what happened here on football. You simply have to think of the thousands of schools in this country that have football teams, and where nothing like this has ever happened. What happened here goes much deeper.

—Beth Bender

I think Brendan got it worse than the other kids. Like you'd see a crowd of guys talking to some girls but intentionally blocking the hall, you know? Like asserting their power. Trying to impress the girls, or whatever. Some kids would see that and just, you know, try to find another way around or wait until the crowd broke up, even if it meant they'd be late. But Brendan couldn't stand it. He knew what they were doing, and it just made him nuts. Some jocks are saying that Brendan went out of his way to start fights, but I don't think it was that. I think he just felt really strongly that he had a right to go down the hall and that it was wrong for those guys to block it just to prove they owned the place.

—Dustin Williams

The chicken!&*# teachers know what's going on. Today friggin' Flach shoved me in the hall and called me a faggot right in front of Mr. Ellin. You know that jerk Ellin? He's a new biology teacher. I think this is his first year. He's one of those preppies in Gap chinos and a blue button-down shirt. Halfway between student and teacher. So he tells me I shouldn't take it personally. Can you friggin' believe it? I get slammed and dissed, and I'm not supposed to take it personally? I mean, why didn't he drag Flach's butt down to [Principal] Curry's office?

These stupid teachers, you know? Especially the new, young ones. They think they're like you. Like you've got something in common. Like I'd ever want to be a friggin' teacher.

So, you'll love this. Ellin tells me it's all genetics. The athletes are the dominant males, and they're driven by their friggin' genes to keep the rest of the pack in line. Like the next time one of them smashes my face into the friggin' lockers, I'm supposed to forgive him because he's not really doin' it, it's his friggin' genes making him do it.

I mean, who gives a rat's ass why they do it? What the hell difference does it make? You think some loser getting his butt whipped really gives a flying #$*% whether the guy who's doing it personally hates his guts or is just being driven by some friggin' chromosome? Gimme a break. When I take 'em out, I'm gonna make sure I nail this guy Ellin just because he tried to give it a reason. Like an excuse or something. Like he thinks maybe on some level that makes it understandable. If that's understandable, so's popping a cap in his ass with a friggin' TEC-9.

—an e-mail from Brendan to Gary

The boys call each other a few names, and in no time, unless one of them backs down, they're fighting. It's different with girls. It's all backbiting and nastiness. The

"How many kids ostracized, humiliated, and assaulted in American high schools, like the survivors of Columbine High, are left scarred for life? How many commit suicide every year? So long as some kids go out of their way to make high school hell for others, there are going to be kids who crack, and not all of the kids who crack are going to quietly off themselves."
—a posting on the Internet

popular girls wouldn't dream of fighting. They might chip a nail. They fight with words and looks and searing little offhand comments designed to cut your heart out. Everyone wants to be young again, but each time I see these girls reduce someone to tears, it makes me think twice.

—Beth Bender

Maybe we stereotype them, but they stereotype us, too. To them we're all big dumb jocks. They seem to forget that Dustin Williams's GPA is way up there, and so are a couple of other guys'. And who says they don't want to be stereotyped? If you walk around this school putting it down and dissing on sports and spirit, aren't you kind of just asking to be stereotyped?

—Paul Burns, football player

You're walking down the hall, minding your own business. You see this guy, and he just sneers at you and says, "Hey, faggot." Thing is, to him it's nothing. Two seconds later he's probably forgotten he even said it. But it's burned in your brain. It's a permanent scar. A week later you're still asking yourself, why'd he have to do that? Why'd he have to pick you? Does everyone think you're a faggot? Maybe you are a faggot and you don't even know it.

It's like torture. You know "Sticks and stones will break

More than 50 percent of male youths say it would be easy to obtain a gun.

my bones, but names will never hurt me"? It's a load of crap. A stick stops hurting after a few minutes. Names last a long time.

—Ryan Clancy

I was talking with Brendan in the hall, and Sam Flach came by and gave him just the slightest nudge. The sort of harmless thing that must happen a thousand times a day in a crowded school like ours. At first I thought Brendan overreacted. Making a fist, muttering under his breath. I stupidly said, "Oh, come on, Brendan, it wasn't that bad, just a little push." Brendan looked back at me with such hurt in his eyes. He said, "No, Ms. Bender, it's not 'just' a little push, not when it happens every day." Even then I didn't take it that seriously. But now I think I understand. What if it really was constant, unrelenting torment? A little bit of salt doesn't bother your skin. But that same small amount in an open wound can really, really sting.

—Beth Bender

It wasn't just in the halls. It was everywhere. Once, in gym, we were out in the field a couple of days after a big rain. The grass had pretty much dried, but there were still a few puddles. Next thing I know, [Sam] Flach and [Paul]

"I went to three [high schools], and in none of [them] did I for a moment feel safe. High school was terrifying, and it was the casual cruelty of the popular kids that made it hell."

—a posting on the Internet

Burns push me down. Each one grabs a leg, and they drag me through a couple of muddy puddles. I'm drenched with grimy water and smeared with mud, and Bosco comes over, and I swear he's having a really hard time not grinning. He tells Flach and Burns to let go and tells me to go clean up. And that was it. I mean, it was almost like he was giving those guys a license to do it again anytime they liked.

—Ryan Clancy

Everyone thinks about suicide when they're a teenager. At least, almost everyone I know. It's just, like, something really crappy happens and you're in this horrible pain, and what's the point? Gary loved that old Queen song, the one they sang in the car in *Wayne's World*. You know, where the singer says he shot someone in the head and his life is ruined, but nothing really matters anyway. I mean, don't take this the wrong way and think you've made some big discovery. He didn't do what he did because of some stupid song.

—Allison Findley

Lots of kids'll say they want to kill themselves at one point or another, but Gary would really go into detail about it. I remember he once got into this whole thing

---

The presence of a gun in the home increases the risk of suicide fivefold.

"By state or region . . . for every age, for both genders, where there are more guns, there are more total suicides."
—National Center for Biotechnology Information

about hanging himself from the flagpole in front of the school. So you'd get to school the next morning, and instead of the flag, there'd be Gary. The thing of it was he couldn't figure out how to do it. Like, how would he get up there? He thought maybe a really long extension ladder would do the trick. I figured it was just typical Gary stuff, but a couple of days later we were leaving school, and he actually took off his backpack and tried to shimmy up the flagpole. Of course he couldn't. But it really hit me: Two days later and he's still thinking about it.

—Ryan Clancy

I can't begin to count how many times on a Saturday around noon I'd knock on Gary's door and find him still in bed, wide awake, simply lying there with that thick quilt wrapped around him like a cocoon. I'd suggest that he go outside, find someone to do something with. He'd always say he would "in a moment." But sometimes he wouldn't get out of bed until three or four. I always felt as if there was something inside keeping him from being happy and active like other boys. A lead curtain of sadness that was too heavy for him to lift. I'm sure it had to do with the divorce. I can't tell you how many times I'd see him like that, then go into my own room and just cry.

—Cynthia Searle

This one night I came home pretty late. It was definitely after midnight. Brendan was sitting in the dark on the curb in front of his house. Elbows on his knees, his head hung. Looking pretty bummed. So I went over and asked if everything was okay. He said no as if it was obvious things weren't okay. I guess it was a dumb question, so I apologized. He patted the curb next to him. You know, have a seat.

I sat down. You could smell the liquor on him, and I think I might have said something about drinking alone. He got into this rap about how we were both minorities, him being an outcast and me being African American. And didn't I know that if it weren't for football, I'd be in the same boat as him? I told him I thought there might be some truth to that, but that while there were definitely some bigots around, the majority of people we knew were smart enough to know better.

He asked if I knew that some of the worst bigots in school were on the team. I said I didn't think that was the case. We talked a little more, and then I got up and said I had to get to bed. Practice the next day, you know? I asked if he was going in, and he shook his head and said he was going to stay out for a while more. He tried to be tough and cool, but right at that moment he looked mostly miserable and weak.

"Most of the attackers in the recent cases had shown signs of clinical depression or other psychological problems. But schools, strapped for mental health counselors, are less likely to pick up on such behavior or to have the available help."

—New York Times, 6/14/98

Since we'd been talking pretty intimately, I asked him why he was doing this to himself. You know, drinking alone and fighting and generally making himself an outsider. He just looked up at me. Maybe it was my imagination, but I thought his eyes were glistening, like with tears. And then he said that if I weren't on the team, I'd want to kill each and every one of them too. I said I was sorry but I didn't see it that way.

—Dustin Williams

If you're going to teach ninth-grade English, you have to be prepared for some off-the-wall stuff, especially from a kid like Brendan Lawlor. You see kids like him every year. You get the feeling they're at war in their mind, fighting some constant battle inside themselves as well as with everyone around them. Brendan wrote poems that sounded like plots for nightmarish action movies. Poems about automatic-weapons fire, limbs being torn off, the smell of burning flesh, skulls crushed and brains splattered in the halls, bombs, people begging for mercy before having their throats slit, then blowing yourself away. You would almost assume it was satire, except that for a kid like Brendan it was deadly serious. There were times when you wanted to take him by the shoulders and shake him. *Come on, wake up! You're*

In 2016 the United States led all high-income countries in firearm deaths among its youth. The rate in the US was 36.5 times higher than in a dozen comparable countries.

—CNN

young. You've got your whole life ahead of you. Buckle down, work hard, go on a date, go to college, and get on with it.

—Dick Flanagan,
Brendan's ninth-grade English teacher
at Middletown High School

PART OF BRENDAN'S SUICIDE NOTE

Know what? Not everybody has to do what you A-holes want them to do. Maybe your kids did, but me and my friends chose not to. And you and your kids couldn't deal with that. And so you had to do what stupid, ignorant people always do when they don't understand—you had to attack and torment us.

And you teachers. I thought you taught us that America is supposed to be about freedom. Kids are supposed to be able to be different without the status quo police smashing us over the head and ridiculing us. But that's all you teachers did to me and my friends. Just like everyone else, you tried to make us conform to your narrow-minded expectations of how we were supposed to dress and act.

Well, screw you. Screw all of you. I hope this letter is like a knife in your hearts. You ruined my life. All I've done is pay you back in kind.

More of Ninth Grade

Gary thought it was all a big joke anyway. He always said life was an accident. I mean, life on this planet. It wasn't anything that was meant to be. Most of the time I didn't bother to argue. But sometimes it made me sad. People tell me I'm really angry inside. It's probably true. But at least now I think maybe it can get better. But to Gary it was always hopeless and meaningless.

I think his mom might have been religious. Anyway, I hear she's been going to church a lot since what happened.

—Allison Findley

One day in class we were talking about morality, and Brendan said there was no God. He didn't say that he didn't believe in God. He just said there was no God. Like he had this special knowledge and that was just the way it was, take it or leave it. The whole class went quiet. Even Mr. Flanagan was kind of shocked. He said Brendan could feel that way if he wanted, but that was his opinion and not necessarily the truth. But Brendan, he just kept saying there was no God. Like it wasn't enough to say what he believed. He had to try and force it down everyone else's throat too. I really wanted to pound the crap out of him.

—Paul Burns

It's stupid to point at one incident and say, "It's all because of this." It has to be something that builds gradually and eats at you for a long time until you go psycho. But having said that, I'll tell you about one thing that happened in ninth grade that really changed Brendan. It was the time they did the swirly to him. They held him by the ankles and dunked his head in the toilet. It was all over school in no time. After Gary and I heard about it, we went looking for [Brendan], but he was gone.

—Ryan Clancy

Face it, there are two sets of rules: one for those who are in favor and one for those who aren't. If Deirdre Bunson is talking in world history, it's like, "Excuse me, Deirdre, now pay attention." But if Allison Findley is talking, Ms. Arnold stops the class and stares at her. And then the rest of the kids stare at her. It's a light slap on the wrist for Deirdre. It's public humiliation for Allison.

—Allison Findley

[Brendan] called me the second night. I said, "Brendan, where have you been [for the past two days]?" He said he'd been ditching. He couldn't face anyone at school. I asked why he didn't tell his parents or the school, and he just laughed. He said if the guys who did [the swirly]

Several people said immediately after the shooting that Michael Carneal was an atheist, or at least had associated with atheists.

found out [he'd told on them], it would only make it worse. He went to school the next day and got two weeks' detention for unexplained absence. Is that fair?

—Emily Kirsch

Everybody's looking for someone to blame. So, of course, since I'm on the [football] team and I had some scrapes with those guys, a lot of people want to blame me. Let me tell you something. I'm not going to deny that I mixed it up with them. I did it, and I'm not proud of it. Obviously, after what they did to me, I'm gonna regret it for as long as I live. But there's just one thing. It wasn't like I went looking for them. Those guys, especially Brendan, it was like he always wanted to start something. Like he went out of his way to ask for it.

—Sam Flach

Like all other animals, we are born with instincts and a genetic blueprint of what we must do to survive. The big difference is that humans possess the potential for becoming civilized, thinking, *reasoning* creatures. Eventually we are supposed to learn to suppress our animal instincts in order to meld with the society around us.

But at what point is the process of suppressing our animal

Approximately 39,773 Americans were killed by firearms in homicides, suicides, and accidents in 2017. In comparison, during the three years of the Korean War, 33,651 Americans were killed. During nearly eight years of the war in Vietnam, 58,148 Americans were killed.

instincts complete? Seven years of age? Fourteen? Twenty-one? In other words, do we expect too much of teenagers?

—F. Douglas Ellin,
a biology teacher at Middletown High School

I suppose I'm as much at fault as anyone. But it's not like football players are monsters. Kids have been getting into fights and picking on one another since forever. I don't know why Brendan and Gary did what they decided to do, but to say it was all because some football players picked on them has to be a gross oversimplification.

—Dustin Williams

There is an unwritten law here about the treatment of athletes, especially those athletes on the teams that have a chance to go to the playoffs and bring the school recognition and enhance its pride. In our case, that's football and wrestling. The [unwritten] law states that you may discipline a student athlete up to a point. But it must be an absolutely extraordinary situation for you to do anything that would impinge on that athlete's ability to play for his team. To do so would be to invite the worst kind of scorn, not just from the football coaches, but from the administration, other teachers, and the town at large. Do a few of the athletes know this and take advantage of it? What do you think?

—Beth Bender

With the trend toward two parents working and spending less time at home, the responsibility for raising children and instilling them with values rests more and more on the shoulders of the schools. We are no longer supposed to teach just academics; we are now supposed to rear, nurture, coddle, protect, encourage, discipline, and teach good hygiene and eating habits. If you're a teacher with six classes of roughly thirty kids each, how exactly are you supposed to do that?

—Allen Curry,
principal of Middletown High School

My mother says I'm a pack rat. I save everything. I don't know why, I just do. Gary, Brendan, Allison, and I would get into a chat room and shoot the breeze, and if I thought it was interesting, I'd save it onto a Zip drive. As soon as the cops found out, they got a warrant and came in here and took it all away, but my dad went to court and got some of it back after the cops made copies. After what happened, I went back and started to look at some of the stuff. I thought this one was pretty interesting. Brendan is TerminX. Gary is Dayzd. Allison is Blkchokr, and I'm Rebooto.

—Ryan Clancy

TerminX: Burns called me a nerd 2day.
Blkchokr: Feeble
Rebooto: That's the best he could come up with!
Dayzd: Know what he'll call a nerd 10 years from now?

TerminX: Boss
Rebooto: LOL!
TerminX: It's BS.
Blkchokr: Y?
TerminX: Jocks go 2 college and play on teams. They're heroes.
Rebooto: They get hot babes.
Dayzd: They get babes hot.
TerminX: They study accounting and pre-law. Then they screw up their knees and their career is over. But it doesn't matter.
Blkchokr: Y not?
TerminX: Because they're still winners.
Dayzd: We're losers, with good knees.
Rebooto: Unless U lose Ur knee.
Dayzd: Or Ur knee comes loose.
TerminX: They become partners in accounting firms and law firms, and everyone wants 2 work with them because they were heroes in college.
Blkchokr: Some go into pro sports.
TerminX: It's incredibly rare.
Dayzd: About as rare as some nerd actually being Ur boss.

PART OF GARY'S SUICIDE NOTE

Mom, I could never tell you how unhappy I was. I knew there was nothing you could do to help, and life has been hard enough on you already. I'm truly, truly sorry that I'm going to put you through so much pain, but I hope that in a year or two you'll get over it. Maybe you could move away and change your name and even have a new kid.

You can start over. I wish I could be there with you, but I'm past the point of no return.

The End of Ninth Grade

We talked all the time about getting back at the jocks. For every time they called you a faggot. For every time they bodychecked you into a wall. And every teacher who saw it happen day after day and never did anything more than tell those morons to stop horsing around. We would tie them up and use pliers to pull their fingernails off. We would gouge their eyes out and castrate them. We would burn their noses off with propane torches. I know it must sound sick, but that's how pissed we were. You had these guys breaking the rules and beating on you, and no one tried to stop them.

—Ryan Clancy

Brendan learned I had weapons in the house, because he saw me carrying the case to the car one day when I went [to a gun show]. A few days later he came over and asked about them. I opened the case and let him hold a few. He was certainly surprised at how heavy some of them were. I think he said something to the tune of "I can't believe they're real."

—Jack Phillips,
a neighbor of Brendan's

I will kill every friggin' one of them. It's gonna be Columbine all over again, only better. Harris and Klebold did it right. Blow the friggin' school, then blow yourself away. I wish I could have met them. Maybe we'll go underground after Middletown. Help other outcasts kill the A-hole jocks at their schools. Or die trying. This is the new revolution. This is John Friggin' Brown telling the country we've had enough of this crap. This is one for the history books. Keep fighting until they bring you down in a hail of bullets. Mark my words, Littleton was just the beginning.

—an e-mail from Brendan to Gary

The first gun Brendan got he bought from this kid in school. The thing is, if you know anything about this stuff, [the gun he bought] was a piece of crap. I think it was made in Brazil or someplace. Brendan said he paid a hundred [dollars] for it, and I heard someone say that the kid who sold it to him had bought it for, like, thirty. But Brendan didn't care. All he cared about was having that gun.

—Ryan Clancy

Brendan was changing. Definitely getting darker and angrier, although sometimes he'd be the old Brendan, funny and charming and goofy. It was probably about a month after they did the swirly on him when he called up and said he wanted to go up to the park. Usually we'd just sit under a tree near the parking lot and talk and drink, but this time there was someplace he really wanted to get to. You could tell there was something on his mind. We got into the park, and he was like, "Let's go up on the hill." It's a big hill, and Gary and I were really huffing and puffing. I have to quit smoking. We got up there, and he took this gun out of his pocket. Like, first we thought it was a toy, then Gary thought maybe a starter's pistol. Brendan said it was real, and I asked what he was going to do with it. I won't use the words he used, but basically he said he was going to blow away some kids at school.

—Allison Findley

My dad has a 9 mm Glock he keeps on a shelf in his bedroom closet. It's got that nice black finish like the ones you see on TV. When we used to go on camping trips, he'd put it in the glove compartment of our car. The thing is, I know some kids who really have arsenals—like rifles, shotguns, and pistols. I'm not talking about their fathers. I'm talking about them. Although their fathers have lots of guns too. So when Brendan showed me this gun he'd bought, I was pretty much, are you for real? I think he thought I was surprised he had a gun, but I was like, "Give me a break, that's not a gun, it's a toy." Man, I wish I hadn't said that.

—Ryan Clancy

In 1998, according to federal estimates, there were about 280 million people and 240 million guns in America. By 2018 those numbers had increased to 328 million people and 393 million guns.

Have you ever noticed how the staff wear their walkie-talkies on their hip? I know that's the logical place for them, but I can't help thinking of the similarity to the sheriff and his deputies in the Wild West. The way they're so quick to point that walkie-talkie at kids who are misbehaving. As if it's loaded with communication bullets. *If you don't respect my authority, I'll call in the reinforcements.* When I was in school, the principal didn't carry a walkie-talkie. He didn't need one. We respected his authority. Or we feared it. You can say the staff need their walkie-talkies because there's no respect for authority anymore. But perhaps there would be respect if the staff weren't so quick to rely on threats. I don't know. Anyway, it probably doesn't even matter. It's probably too late now to change.

—Beth Bender

[Brendan] was very interested, very respectful. He wouldn't touch a gun unless he asked first. But he was fascinated by them. He had to pick up each one, get the feel of it, sight it. You know, the very same things gun people do. He was a natural.

—Jack Phillips

Gary asked me if I would get him a gun. He'd prepared his argument very carefully. Lots of kids had guns. He'd

---

Virtually all of the semiautomatic pistols manufactured in Brazil are exported because Brazilian law forbids civilian ownership of such guns. (*Making a Killing*)

take a safety course. It was for target practice only. I said I didn't believe in having guns. As far as I was concerned, there was no place in our home for one. I'd be lying if I said it didn't cross my mind that he might use it on himself.

—Cynthia Searle

You know how sometimes you go to a movie and you come out and for a little while you sort of feel like one of the characters? Maybe you even talk like them? Brendan, Gary, and I went to one of these dumb horror movies. There's a scene where the killer guy picks up one of his victims and throws him off an overpass, right in front of a big truck going underneath.

So, it's night and we were walking home, and Brendan stops on the overpass and watches the cars going by underneath. He just stood there. Gary and I called to him to come on, but he wouldn't. We didn't know what he was doing. All of a sudden he starts to throw something. It turned out he wasn't throwing anything, just going through the motion. But it looked like it to us, and to the cars underneath. There's this horrible screeching and squealing of tires, and you knew cars were skidding and swerving to get out of the way, and you're sure any second you're going to hear a crash, but it didn't happen.

Among students who said they carried a gun, 53 percent said they had obtained the gun from home or family; 37 percent obtained the gun "off the street."

I wanted to run, get out of there before someone came up and caught us. But Brendan wouldn't run. He just walked up to us with a big smile on his face and said, didn't we think that was the wicked coolest thing?

—Allison Findley

Whatever that dark thing in Brendan was, it started to come out in Gary, too. I always thought of Gary as more lost and sad than angry. I mean, I don't know whether what Gary had came from Brendan, or whether Brendan just brought it out in Gary. I hate to say this, but maybe it would have come out in Gary even if Brendan hadn't been there. But the two of them together . . . I don't know, they just fed off each other.

—Emily Kirsch

Allison [Findley] worried me too. She came to school in dirty clothes, with dirty hair, and sometimes, to be blunt, she smelled. I was concerned for her, both because I wondered if there was something wrong at home, and because of the way the other girls treated her. She was a bit overweight, but also very well developed. You would hear things. I had no way of knowing if they were true. I hoped they weren't.

—Beth Bender

"Mitchell Johnson's mother . . . said . . . that she taught her boy how to shoot a shotgun, and then he took a three-week course."

—*New York Times, 6/14/98*

We hear all the time about the supposed deterioration of the behavior of young people over the past thirty years. Can we really put a value judgment on it? Maybe the behavior of teenagers has changed, but I'm not sure that implies deterioration. We read that with parents working so much and grandparents off in their retirement villages, there are far fewer adults around to influence youngsters. The articles do make one interesting point—that in the absence of real adult role models, violent television and video images have become the substitute role models. I think that's probably true.

—F. Douglas Ellin

At the request of the police, Dick Flanagan and I went back and collected some of [Gary's and Brendan's] writings. We were both struck by how certain themes came out, not necessarily in any one piece of writing, but in the body of work as a whole. It was clear that Gary felt weak and defenseless. He wrote often about characters who were teased and picked on. The themes in Brendan's writings were less clear but much more aggressive. More like you were in some extremely violent video game. The characters in his stories were always getting revenge, always on the attack with weapons capable of terrible destruction.

—Allen Curry

Brendan was seriously into [first-person shooter video games]. If you want to know the truth, so were a lot of other kids who didn't do what he did. But one day Gary and I are in his room with him, just hacking around on the computer and listening to music, and Brendan's like, "Point and click, point and click!" Like he's just figured something out, you know? So he goes crawling into his closet and comes out with that crappy little gun, and he aims it at me. I guess he saw the look on my face, because he said, "Don't worry, it's not loaded." Then he dry-fires the [gun] and it goes *click,* and he says, "See? Point and click! It's the same thing!"

—Ryan Clancy

No one is naive enough to believe that violent movies or television or video games *can actually make* anyone commit a violent act. The real question is, If someone is inclined toward violence, do these forms of media help show him the way to do it?

—F. Douglas Ellin

Brendan got into this "point and click" thing for a while. At lunch he'd put his arm on the table and plant his chin behind it so it looked like he was peeking over a wall. Then he'd stick his thumb up and point his finger at the kids he hated. He'd go, "Point and click, point and click. Die suckas." Like he was picking them off one by one.

—Allison Findley

The average twelve-year-old has seen more than eight thousand murders on TV. By the time they reach 18, that number has increased to 200,000.

This one was after that school shooting in Idaho.

—Ryan Clancy

TerminX: Gun control is friggin' stupid. Gunz don't kill people. People kill people.

Rebooto: But if people can't get gunz . . .

TerminX: They find a way.

Dayzd: My granddad's from WY. Everyone has gunz. U get a .22 at 10 and hunt squirrels.

Blkchokr: Y?

TerminX: Y what?

Blkchokr: Y hunt squirrels?

Dayzd: Eat them.

TerminX: U never 8 squirrel?

Blkchokr: Gross, and neither have U, Trm.

Dayzd: How come when my granddad was a kid, kids didn't go 2 school and kill people?

Rebooto: MayB they nu it was wrong.

TerminX: U think Klebold and Harris didn't know it was wrong in Littleton?

Rebooto: Then Y?

Dayzd: Nothing better 2 do.

TerminX: K&H didn't care. Want 2 know what's different between now and 50 years ago? Back then kids cared.

Several studies have shown that the appearance on television and in the movies of semiautomatic guns like the Bren 10 and TEC-9 boosted sales of those weapons. (*Making a Killing*)

Blkchokr: What about?

Dayzd: Santa Clauz.

TerminX: They believed in crap. Don't ask me what, 'cause whatever it was is gone now. Back then U had a reason not 2 kill people.

Blkchokr: U don't now?

Dayzd: Lethal injection.

Rebooto: Milky Ways.

TerminX: No 1 cares anymore. No 1 believes. Nothing 2 care about. Nothing 2 believe in.

Dayzd: I believe in love.

Rebooto: I'm dyslexic. I believe in doG.

TerminX: We're all gonna die. MayB I'll die before U, but sooner or later U'll croak 2.

Blkchokr: Duh.

Dayzd: I won't die.

Rebooto: I'll come back as an amoeba.

TerminX: Once U're dead, U're gone and 4gotten. But it'll be a long time before they 4get about Littleton.

Dayzd: Huh?

Sales of the semiautomatic AK-47 assault rifles increased dramatically after Patrick Edward Purdy used one to kill five children and wound thirty more on a school playground in California. Studies have repeatedly shown that gun purchases often spike after a mass shooting because buyers fear that the event will prompt stricter gun control legislation. (*Lethal Passage*)

Blkchokr: Trm, U think that's Y they did it? 2 B remembered?

TerminX: It's part of it. Remember Jesse James? Al Capone?

Blkchokr: Attila the Hun. Hitler.

Rebooto: That creep who 8 people.

Dayzd: Dahmer.

Blkchokr: Impressed, Dayz.

Dayzd: I can C it, Trm. The combo plate. Get the buttholes who make Ur life miserable. Plus Ur name in history. And "nothing really matters . . . to me."

TerminX: Starts 2 look good. U get them. They get what they deserve. Plus U're famous.

Dayzd: Infamous.

Rebooto: Like President Clinton!

Blkchokr: O. J. Simpson.

Dayzd: Michael Jackson.

Rebooto: That's sick.

TerminX: 13 kids went down in Littleton. Who do U remember?

Violent events are often covered by news outlets in great detail and spread through mass and social media. Experts believe that this media coverage can inspire others to copy these actions. This is called the media contagion effect. Before 2000 there were about three mass shootings *per year*. In 2018 there were approximately 323 mass shootings in the United States: *Nearly one per day*. A mass shooting is generally defined as one in which at least four people are wounded or killed in one incident.

Dayzd: Klebold and Harris.
TerminX: I rest my case.

At the end of ninth grade we had this awards assembly. It was for everything, not just sports. I was sitting with the guys on the [football] team. Principal Curry announced the awards for the speech and debate team, and these kids started to go up on stage. So, you know, these were the brainy kids, and some of them looked okay, but a couple of them were wearing thick glasses and had funny builds. So the guys on the football team start booing. It was just plain stupid. I recall I actually felt embarrassed. I think I even bent my head down so people would see that I wasn't one of them. But it was like a glimpse at how those other kids must have felt, you know? Could you imagine the speech and debate team booing when the football players got their awards? There would be a massacre.

—Dustin Williams

Shooters get enormous attention: their names, photos, motivations, and stories are often shared on media for days following the event. The American Psychological Association points out that this "fame" is something that most mass shooters desire, and sometimes inspires a copycat shooting, where the potential shooter tries to kill more people than their predecessor.
—National Center for Health Research

Tenth Grade

We moved to Middletown at the end of ninth grade, so tenth grade was my first year here. It's so different from my old school. You expect it to be different, but what surprised me was the way it was different. It's just a lot more rigid here. It's like, are you in the popular crowd or not? There was a popular crowd at my old school too, but they were still nice to most people. They didn't act like if you weren't one of them you didn't deserve to exist.

I remember coming home after the first week and telling my mom I didn't like it. Some of the kids just weren't nice at all. They'd push and curse in the hall, and it didn't seem like any of the teachers really went out of their way to stop it. Mom said to lie low. I've always been pretty good at making friends, and she knew I'd find some at Middletown High. She said I only had

"'There has never . . . been a cohort of kids that is so little affected by adult guidance and so attuned to a peer world. . . . We have removed grown-up wisdom and allowed [children] to drift into a self-constructed, highly relativistic world of friendship and peers.'"
—Prof. William Damon, Stanford University,
New York Times, 10/3/99

three years to go. I remember thinking it sounded like an eternity.

—Chelsea Baker,
a transfer student to Middletown High School

One thing I don't think a lot of people on the outside realize is how incredibly hard a football team trains. The hours of practice on the weekdays and weekends. Learning forty or fifty plays in your playbook, plus each week studying the films of the team you're facing that Friday night. On top of that you've got schoolwork. And the weight and strength training you have to do on your own just to survive out there. The pressure is huge, and to be honest, there are guys who . . . well, the only way they have to blow off steam is fighting.

—Dustin Williams

I always felt Brendan and I had a special connection, even after the point, around the beginning of tenth grade, when we didn't talk much anymore. Maybe it went back to seventh grade, when we were both new. Maybe it was because we were both quote, unquote "outcasts." Anyway, you know how Brendan always seemed to attract trouble. There was just something about him. Every slight, real or imagined, made his fur go up. And he couldn't back down. I mean, it wasn't like he was trying to prove how tough he was. I really think there was something in him. He was helpless to resist it. Even when he was scared silly, he had to stand up to it.

—Emily Kirsch

A lot of what they're saying about the football players is a load of crap. So what if we wore our jerseys to school on game days? All we were doing was trying to get some school spirit going. I've got news for you. You're out there on the field banging heads with some 220-pound lineman for four quarters, you need some support from the stands. But it wasn't like it was a rule. If you didn't want to have school spirit, that was your business. But some of those guys went further than that. It was like they wanted to destroy school spirit.

—Sam Flach

It's important that you look at this realistically. The issue of school spirit is certainly a factor in the tensions between these two groups of kids, but you have to believe it's been blown out of proportion. You're not going to have cheerleaders for the chess team. You're not going to fill the bleachers with fans who cheer when a kid from Middletown takes his opponent's rook. Even the chess players don't want that. Of course we want to produce scholars and we take pride in our National Honor Society members. But that's a matter of school pride, and it's different from school spirit.

—Dick Flanagan

In the 40 years between 1960 and 2000, roughly 750,000 people in this country died from gun violence. At current rates, the number of gun deaths in *the next* 40 years will be roughly twice that: 1.5 million.

When you're with someone a lot, they can change, but it's gradual, so you're not always aware of it. I think that's what happened to all of us, but more to Brendan. Looking back on it, I realize he just got weirder and more and more twisted. It was like he stopped caring. He'd do whatever he wanted.

There was one night when Gary wasn't around. I think maybe he had to go see some psychologist with his mom. Brendan called up and wanted to go out. I'm older than most of the kids in my grade and I have a license, so I usually drive. Anyway, I supplied the car and Brendan supplied the booze. It was probably screwdrivers. We went up to the park and drank for a while and talked. I can't remember now what we talked about, but with Brendan it was usually about how much he hated school and town and blah, blah, blah. Sometimes when I had a good buzz going, I could just tune him out.

After a while Brendan wanted to get in the car again. We drove out of the park, and I thought we'd head back toward town, but he wanted to go the other way. The other way is basically nowhere. Just dark roads and farms and hills, but by then I was pretty trashed and couldn't have cared less.

We're driving along this road way out in the country, and it's a pretty cool night, so I'm kind of surprised when Brendan rolls down the window.

I guess I was sort of aware that he took something out of his jacket. When I heard the bang, I thought one of the tires had blown out or Brendan had thrown a firecracker out of the window. That's what it sounded like. Not really loud or anything. Then we came to the railroad crossing. The red lights were blinking and the gates were coming down, and out of the corner of my eye there's a bright flash and I hear *Bang! Bang!* Only it's louder because we're stopped, and then there's the sound of glass shattering. That's when I realized Brendan was shooting at things.

Bang! Bang! He shot out the other light. You know the smell of burned gunpowder? Then he looked across the seat at me and smiled. I was beyond caring. The railroad gates went up, and we kept driving. Brendan kept shooting. Mostly at signs. Then he opened the glove compartment so he had light while he put more bullets in the clip, or whatever they call it. The gun looked bigger and squarer than the one he'd showed us that time in the park.

I never said a word. I didn't tell him to stop. I didn't turn around and go back to town. To be honest, I just didn't care. I actually thought it was a little cool. Like we were a couple of outlaws on the run in *Natural Born Killers.*

After a while it was late and we did head back to town. By the time we got to Brendan's, just about every house on his street was dark. Everyone was asleep. Brendan and I sat for a while in the car. You could still smell the

---

Twelve percent of students say they *know* another student who has brought a gun to school. Five percent say they've actually seen the gun.

gunpowder. I realized that since we'd started driving, he'd hardly said a word.

He looked across the seat at me again. I hope this doesn't sound sick, but it was a really sexy moment. I mean, he really was an outlaw and dangerous and unpredictable, and I happen to find that extremely attractive. I think he knew that. He started to move toward me, and I'm thinking, *This is my boyfriend's best friend. I don't believe this.* But I really don't think he cared. I really don't.

Anyway, I know this will sound weird after everything I've just said, but I wouldn't let him touch me. I still don't know why. I think maybe it was that dark thing inside him. He could be sexy and attractive, but it was too scary.

—Allison Findley

The school I came from had the same crowds as Middletown. There were athletes and brains and preppies and rah-rah girls and stoners. There were cliques, but they weren't that big of a deal. Sometimes I felt like the real power of a clique was only in the minds of those kids who wished they were in it. If you didn't care, you just went along with your life. At least, at my old school.

—Chelsea Baker

In ninth grade we might have done some drinking once or twice a month and smoked some pot or hash now and then. By tenth grade we were smashed every Friday and Saturday night. We were getting high in school. A couple of times we dropped acid in eighth period so we'd have a nice buzz going by the time school was over. Oh, and I'm not just talking about Brendan, Allison, Gary, and me. This was a lot of kids. Athletes, too.

—Ryan Clancy

I'm not so far from being a teenager myself, and I can tell you that there's a huge amount of denial among parents. Anyone who insists that "my kid isn't drinking, my kid isn't smoking pot, my kid isn't having sex." Maybe they're right. But look at the statistics and you'll know they can't all be right.

—F. Douglas Ellin

TerminX: Ever C a dead person?
Blkchokr: In a casket.
TerminX: What was it like?
Blkchokr: It was my grandma. Not a lot different than when she was alive.
Dayzd: LOL.
Rebooto: You can go C my grandparents, Trm. They're almost dead.
TerminX: I mean it.
Dayzd: What?
TerminX: A dead person. Spark gone. Lifeless flesh.

Of the male youths who say it would be easy to obtain a gun, most say they can get a gun within twenty-four hours.

Blkchokr: I don't want 2 talk about this.
TerminX: Y?
Blkchokr: So what's tomorrow's weather supposed 2 B?
TerminX: Scares U?
Blkchokr: Bothers me.
Dayzd: I can C it.
Rebooto: What's 2 C?
Dayzd: Eternal peace.
Rebooto: Eternal nothingness.
TerminX: Same difference.
Blkchokr: I'm outahere.
Dayzd: Later, Blk.
Rebooto: Bye, Blk.
TerminX: Imagine death.
Dayzd: No pain.
Rebooto: No gain.
TerminX: Insane.

Everything seemed to get more extreme [in tenth grade]. The battle lines became more clearly drawn, you know? I think a lot of things contributed to it. The Middletown Marauders went to the states that fall. It was the furthest a team from Middletown had gone in twenty-five years, and we were feeling pretty full of ourselves. We deserved it, considering how hard we'd worked. But it was kind of like Brendan and Gary were on a campaign to belittle what we'd done. Make it seem as if what we'd accomplished was meaningless and that we were basically just a bunch of dumb jocks with no future. They never said it in words. It was all done with looks and smirks and sniggers. But the football players heard them loud and clear.

—Dustin Williams

The weird thing is this year I actually started to make friends with some of the quote, unquote "popular" girls. I'm not really sure why. I think maybe it happened because I don't judge people and they were sick of being in a crowd where they were judged all the time. Like, how cool is your car and how many free minutes do you get on your cell phone? I mean, who cares?

But sometimes they forget. Like the whole judgment thing is so ingrained in them they can't help it. I have a friend who has lots of piercings and he wears black all the time and he likes heavy metal. I was with him one day in the hall, and my "popular" friends gave me these looks. I saw them later and they were like, "How could you talk to him? How could you even acknowledge his presence?" They just couldn't shake it.

—Emily Kirsch

Our school puts a significant emphasis on sports. I'm in the English department, and you can imagine how it feels when you hear that they've hired a private plane for $25,000 to take the team to a game. Do you have any idea how many classroom sets of Guterson, Shakespeare, and Lowry that would buy? But you also have to understand that a lot of these boys would be lost without athletics.

They are simply never going to be scholars. This is the playing field where they've chosen to compete, and unfortunately it's a lot more expensive than an English classroom. These boys are not studious; many of them will not go to college. A great season here may be the highlight of their life. But even if it isn't, the lessons they learn about work and discipline on the team will serve them well in whatever they do. It just may be that for these boys those lessons are more important than Shakespeare's sonnets.

—Dick Flanagan

At my old school you didn't have this feeling that one crowd was so totally in power and better than all the rest. It was great if you were a super soccer player, but it was pretty cool if you could make your own movie, or draw or act or play the guitar really well. And it was just dumb to put someone down because they got good grades. But here, it's like the only thing that matters is sports. You get straight A's and people dump on you. It doesn't make sense.

—Chelsea Baker

Running a school is like running a business. I know this may sound crass, but you're producing a product. In our case, that product is a high school senior who is prepared to go on in the world and be successful in the community. So, in a way, you can say that we have to produce a product that the community approves of, that they will buy into. Sure, I would love to be Edward James Olmos in *Stand and Deliver* and produce a bunch of kids who value calculus over athletics, but if that's not what the community wants, I'll be out of a job.

—Allen Curry

Being on the football team made you special, and some guys definitely took advantage of that. They'd be late for class or curse right in front of a teacher, even in front of an administrator, and nothing serious would happen. Some of these guys acted like they ruled the school. It affected the way a lot of kids looked at us, especially the younger kids. It was like, "Hey, if I make the team, I can get away with that stuff too." Be honest, deep down inside, who doesn't want to be in the spotlight? Who doesn't want to see their picture in the *Middletown Reporter*? It was a real temptation, and if you wanted to take advantage of it, you could have a great life. Believe me, it was a lot harder not to get a swelled head than to let yourself have one.

—Dustin Williams

They talked about guns and they talked about bombs. Gary and I were in McDonald's once and someone left a newspaper on the table, and there was something about bombing an abortion clinic in it. So Gary's like, "How do they do it?"

And I'm like, "How do they do what?"

And he says, "Make those bombs."

So I go, "Maybe they go to bomb school."

A couple of days later he said he wanted to go to the public library. And I'm like, "What for?"

And he's like, "I want to look at some books, maybe go online."

And I'm like, "You can do that at home." But he says he has to do it at the library. I think he said something about not wanting anyone to trace it back to his computer. He could be a little strange.

We're in the library, and I'm over by the magazines, looking at all these stupid pictures of skinny, perfect girls with perfect hair and skin. It makes you wonder why all the rest of us don't just crawl in some hole and do the world a favor and die. Anyway, Gary comes by with this big grin on his face, and I go, "What?"

And he's like, "Not here. Outside."

We get outside and he starts laughing, like, "You can't believe this, Allison. I found everything I need to know."

"Need to know about what?" I ask.

And he goes, "About making a bomb. Right in the good old library."

In 1990 the Colt firearms company was on the brink of going out of business. One of the reasons was that federal officials had banned the production of the company's AR-15 semiautomatic assault rifle. Hundreds of jobs would be lost if the company closed. The state of Connecticut used state pension funds to purchase 47 percent of the company and save it from going bankrupt. Colt used the money to market a new, slightly modified version of the assault rifle, now called the Sporter.

I'm not sure which he thought was cooler: the fact that he found the information, or the fact that he found it in the library.

—Allison Findley

Everyone's painting this picture of Brendan being the leader and Gary following, but there's another side to it. Especially where those pipe bombs are concerned. Brendan wasn't mechanical. I mean, he just wasn't interested in that kind of thing. But Gary loved building stuff. He really had a talent for it. I remember going to his house for a birthday party and seeing what he'd done with LEGOs. He'd made LEGO robots and programmed them with his computer, so if they walked into something, they could turn around and go in another direction. It was pretty awesome. You hear the police reports about how well constructed and intricate those pipe bombs were. I guarantee you, that was Gary's work.

—Ryan Clancy

I had to take him to the hardware store and over the state line, where they sell fireworks. When we got to the [fireworks] stand, that was probably about the most excited I'd ever seen him. He wanted to know which ones had the

---

"It is the wisdom and judgment of the [Connecticut State] General Assembly that the Sporter is an assault rifle—it's just the AR-15 with a different name."
—Rep. Robert Godfrey

most gunpowder. They told him, and those were the ones he bought.

—Allison Findley

Brendan and Gary had this big announcement they wanted to make. They were going to announce it on Saturday. So Allison drives up and Gary's in the front seat and Brendan's in the back, and we just take off. Listening to music, smoking, cruising. We probably drive for more than an hour and a half, until we're way out in the middle of nowhere. Then we go down some dirt road, and we're at this cabin. I thought Gary said it was his uncle's, but anyway, no one's around.

So Gary opens the trunk and takes out this green duffel bag and all these big sheets of colored paper, like the kind you do school projects on. And we all go tromping off into the woods. The thing is I have no idea what's going on. I'm like, "So what are we doing today? An art project?" And they're not telling me. It's an announcement, you know? I'm supposed to wait.

We get to some place that Gary likes, and he stops and says, "Okay, we'll do it here." Next thing I know, he's taking pushpins out of the duffel bag, and we're supposed to pin all these sheets of paper up to these trees. Like we're making a multicolored room in the trees that's all paper

"We say we want to regulate assault guns; then we go out and buy an assault gun factory. . . . The whole darn thing is so hypocritical it's hard to imagine."

—Rep. David Oliver Thorp

walls. This probably takes an hour itself. And then Gary has to very carefully number all the sheets and make notes in a notebook. I have no idea what this is about, but so what? It's as good as doing anything else, I guess.

Then Gary says we're ready, and he goes back to the bag and he takes out this thing and sets it on the ground right in the middle of the paper room we've created. Then he tells us to get the hell out of there. I ask him how far, and he says a hundred yards at least. If you want to know the truth, I thought he was nuts. A hundred yards is the length of a football field. It's pretty obvious by now that he's got some kind of homemade bomb. But it's kind of fun and goofy to run off into the woods, so I do it.

We go running, and before long we're all bent over with our hands on our knees, gasping for breath. It's the smoking. And a little while later Gary comes crashing through the trees, and we yell to him that we're over here.

The thing goes off before he can get to us. There's this really sharp, loud *thunk!* sound, and I swear a hundred yards away I can actually feel the ground shake and the leaves in the trees rustle. Now Gary and Brendan take off back toward the "blast zone."

So I get there, and I can't believe what I'm seeing. First of all, every single piece of paper is blown away. Totally shredded. It's like a big circle of multicolored paper shreds on the ground around the blast site. Leaves are blown off the trees, so the leaves and paper are mixed together. The whole place reeks of burned gunpowder. Twigs are snapped and some of the smaller branches are broken. You can see that this thing was a lot bigger than it sounded from so far away. Maybe the sound was muffled by the trees and whatnot.

Now Gary says we have to pick up every shred of paper, and he's got rolls of Scotch tape so we can paste them back together. And that's when I figure out what's going on: We're re-creating the scene. Like what they did with that 747 that blew up and they couldn't figure out why.

So now we have to gather up all these little colored shreds of paper and try to tape them together. The thing is maybe you can do it with some of the larger pieces, but the smaller pieces are impossible, and it's not like we haven't been drinking screwdrivers from a plastic half-gallon milk container we brought along.

Finally Brendan says the hell with it. Gary's the only one who doesn't want to stop. If it were up to him, he'd stay out there for a week until every single shred was taped back together. He wants to see the blast pattern, he wants to make sure they built the bomb right. Brendan says, "Look, if we didn't build it right, you think there'd be all this shredded paper and leaves and branches everywhere?"

And Gary's like, "Yeah, but I still want to see." Brendan and I quit and just sit and drink and smoke and watch Allison and Gary pick and tape and pick and tape until even Allison's tired of it. You can see it's hopeless, but Gary is like a fanatic. He just has to see the blast pattern.

Brendan, Allison, and I go back to the cabin, and the door's locked, so Brendan gets the tire iron out of Allison's car and uses it to pry the door open. He pretty much destroys the lock, but we're too trashed to care. We go in and hang around and eat some of the food in the fridge and watch TV. After a while Gary shows up and he's like, okay, he's seen enough. He declares it a success.

He says we should go, and I say, "Well, shouldn't we at least fix the door so your uncle won't have a total fit?" And Gary's like, "Uncle? I don't have any uncle." Can you believe it?

Anyway, we get in the car and start driving back, and all the way they're talking about who they're gonna blow up with these bombs. And it's a pretty good-size list. The only thing is they really meant it.

—Ryan Clancy

TerminX: Pretty awesome 2day, huh? A couple of those suckas in school would put a lot of jerks out of their misery.

Blkchokr: Plus a few non-jerks.

Dayzd: Civilian casualties.

TerminX: Collateral damage.

Rebooto: U guys need 2 make a smart bomb.

Dayzd: Smart bomb 4 dumb jocks.

TerminX: B cool if U could convert that semi-automatic into fully automatic.

Dayzd: Need a hellfire switch.

Rebooto: What R U talking about?

Dayzd: You get a 50-round clip, it's almost the same thing.

TerminX: Jungle-clip them. Then it's 100 rounds.

Rebooto: Hello?

Blkchokr: Gunz, Booto.

Rebooto: :-o

TerminX: I read the marines use a special version of "Doom" 2 train soldiers.

Dayzd: 1-shot kills?

TerminX: Head and upper-torso shots.

Blkchokr: Seen any good movies lately?

Rebooto: Read any good books?

Dayzd: "Unforgiven."

Rebooto: O yeah!

Blkchokr: Weird flick.

Dayzd: Y?

Blkchokr: Couldn't C the message.

TerminX: When a real man has a problem, he gets a gun.

Rebooto: U C where they want 2 expand the movie ratings so they have warnings like cigarettes?

TerminX: Stupid. It doesn't work with cigarettes.

Blkchokr: They're on booze, 2.

Dayzd: Warning: Uncontrolled firearm use may be hazardous to your health.

Blkchokr: LOL!

There are probably about 150 million law-abiding American citizens who enjoy watching football. Myself included. The idea that this incident can somehow be blamed on football is sadly mistaken. These were two sick, disturbed boys. Like many people I know, I also happen to own several hunting rifles and a handgun I keep in my home for personal protection. Is it locked? No, but it's hidden. If I ever have to defend my home against someone trying to break in, the time it takes me to unlock a gun might just be the difference between the life and death of my children.

The Second Amendment to the Constitution gives us the right to bear arms. Are you going to change the Constitution? Why stop at the Second Amendment? Why not throw out the First Amendment, too? Who needs freedom of speech? Hey, who needs the right to vote? See where this is going?

—Dick Flanagan

It's horrible when kids are killed in schools. It's a nightmare. Obviously, after what happened, I should know. But if you want to save kids' lives, you'll save a lot more by raising the driving age than banning guns.

—Allen Curry

It still seems strange to me that I was nobody until Dustin asked me out. I'd be in the girls' room with

---

A gun kept in the home is forty-three times more likely to kill someone you know than to kill a stranger in self-defense. (Lethal Passage)

Deirdre Bunson and some of those other girls, and it was like I didn't even exist. I wasn't on their radar. At my old school you'd say hi to someone even if you didn't know them. Here you say hi and it's like, "Do I know you?"

—Chelsea Baker

I'm sure you've heard about that fight at Dustin's house. If you want to know the truth, up to that point, that was one of the scariest things I'd ever seen. The thing is I always knew [Sam] Flach was mean and strong, but this was just beyond anything you could have imagined.

—Ryan Clancy

I still don't understand why Brendan wanted to go to that party. I mean, he must have felt that Dustin was his neighbor and sort of his friend, but Dustin was on the football team, and everyone knew it was a football party. Some people say Brendan was just asking for it. I don't know. I think it was more like Rosa Parks. He was tired of sitting in the back of the bus.

—Emily Kirsch

We came around the side of the house. You had to go through this gate because Dustin has a pool in his

---

In 1995 there were six states, including the District of Columbia, in which gun-related deaths exceeded traffic fatalities. By 2014 that number had grown to twenty-one states and the District of Columbia.

backyard. Brendan and I were going in. Sam and Deirdre were coming out. The thing is it was just, like, bad timing. Sam got to the gate first. He pushed it open and just kept going. Like he wasn't even going to bother holding it for Deirdre. So Brendan caught the gate and held it for her. Some people say he bowed or touched her on the shoulder or something. I didn't see it. All I saw was Sam come out of nowhere and get Brendan from behind.

—Ryan Clancy

I was in the kitchen and I heard the shouting. I came out, and Sam had Brendan on the ground and was smashing him like a wild animal. There had to be six guys standing around watching. Any one of them could have pulled Sam off, but they didn't. I had to get Sam in a choke hold and practically suffocate him to get him to stop.

—Dustin Williams

Have you ever heard the sound of a fist on bone? It would make you sick. One thing I know for certain, Sam was definitely going for Brendan's face. I swear if I'd had a gun that night, I would have shot Sam myself.

—Ryan Clancy

After Michael Carneal killed three and wounded five in a Paducah, Kentucky, high school, several magazines and newspapers reported that he had imitated a computer-game pattern by quickly shifting from one target to the next.

I went home that night and told my mom there was something really wrong with these kids.

—Chelsea Baker

It wasn't like that in elementary school. I mean, even when two kids got into a fight, they didn't try to hurt each other so badly. Kids in elementary school are way more open to teachers' influence than when they get to middle school and high school. Why can't they teach something in elementary school that could help kids learn how to deal with one another without it always becoming violent?

—Emily Kirsch

I heard about it in the teachers' room first thing Monday morning. A little later I saw Brendan in the hall. His nose was swollen, and his lip was fat and split, and his eye was black and blue. A few minutes later I saw Sam. Not a scratch. You never would've known he'd been in a fight.

—Beth Bender

Boys fight. They've always fought and they always will fight. Was Sam provoked? Who knows. We weren't there.

It was reported that Carneal wounded or killed eight people with eight bullets, despite the fact that he'd never fired a gun before. This was not the case. It was later discovered that Carneal had learned to shoot at a summer camp run by a well-known national youth organization.

We didn't see. Forgive me if I sound callous, but this was an incident that took place off school property.

—Allen Curry

Gary was really down. I didn't know why. It could have been something at home, I'll never know. We were talking on the phone about what happened to Brendan at the party and how the jocks just stood around and didn't stop Sam. Gary said he wished they'd all die. I said, "Not really, right?" He said he really, really did want them to die slow, painful, miserable deaths. I said, "While you live to be a hundred?" He said he really didn't care. He was past the point of caring. He just wanted them to die.

—Allison Findley

Michael Carneal was frequently picked on and teased. The intimation that he was gay was even printed in his school's newspaper. According to several news organizations, Michael Carneal carried a backpack containing more than five hundred rounds of ammunition on the day he killed his fellow students.

The Day It Happened

Brendan called me around dinnertime. It was definitely weird. I don't think we'd spoken on the phone since the end of ninth grade. There was a time when I was pretty sure he was interested in me in a romantic way. But I thought that had passed. Anyway, we talked for a while, and I wasn't sure what he was getting at. Then he told me that about a week before the fight with Sam he'd been rejected by a private military school he'd applied to.

I know that must sound totally out of character. I wonder if Gary even knew. I mean, why in the world would a kid like Brendan want to go to military school? But I think somewhere inside he knew he was headed for big trouble, and he must have believed that military school might be the way to save himself. And if I'm right, then when he was rejected, it was like he lost his last lifeline. Being rejected meant two more years of living hell at Middletown High. I think he knew he'd never survive it.

"Five days before the shooting, Eric [Harris]'s hopes of becoming a marine were undone after his parents told a recruiter about [the antidepressant medicine Eric was taking]. . . . Friends said that Eric was crushed by the news, and had been growing increasingly depressed as graduation neared."

—New York Times, 6/29/99

I think maybe that was the last straw. He lost hope.

We talked for about twenty minutes, and then he asked me if I was going to the dance that night, and I was like, "No way." He asked if I was sure, because he'd noticed that I was getting friendly with some of the quote, unquote "popular" girls. I assured him there was absolutely, positively no way I was going.

And then he said he was glad, and that he'd always liked me. And then he said good-bye.

—Emily Kirsch

I can see how Gary might have been thinking about killing himself. Brendan never struck me that way. It was like he was too angry to do that. He wanted to get too many people. But if you put them together, you can almost see the idea coming to them. Deciding to do themselves in, but going to school and taking as many of those guys with them as they could.

—Ryan Clancy

To me it was just like any other Friday night. The popular kids were at the dance. Gary and Brendan were gone. I

<hr>

Nearly 2,900 American children and teens are killed, and nearly 15,600 injured every year from firearms. That's an average of 51 children and teens per day. The effects of gun violence extend far beyond those struck by a bullet: Such violence shapes the lives of the millions of children who witness it, or who know someone who was shot, or who live in fear of the next shooting.

didn't know where. I went over to Blockbuster. I wasn't really looking for a video. I was looking for someone to hook up with for a couple of hours.

—Allison Findley

It was an unfortunate combination of poor building design and a couple bright minds ingenious enough to take advantage of it. You've got a windowless gym with four main entrances, each consisting of double metal doors. You've got two heavily armed young men who've rigged booby-trap bombs in a way that kept us from getting to the doors from the outside. Inside they chained the doors shut. You want to talk about planning? They brought drinks and snacks for themselves. And flashlights.

—Allen Curry

You hear people say the boys were crazy. That it was just an insane, unpredictable thing that doesn't happen to the vast majority of people. Like getting hit by lightning. Utterly random. But I don't think so. Every year you hear about kids walking into their school and shooting class-mates and teachers. You don't hear about them walking into McDonald's and shooting people. They don't go to the town swimming pool or the movies and do it. Most of these kids live in neighborhoods with elementary

---

Several newspapers reported that Luke Woodham said he killed because he felt he was mistreated every day. He said he did it to show society: "Push us and we will push back."

schools, middle schools, and high schools. But they don't go to some other school. They always go to their own school. It's not random. It's a message, and the sooner we wake up and listen, the better.

—Beth Bender

My father fought in World War Two against the Japanese and the Germans. I realize that it was a long time ago, but when you face a people in mortal combat, it's a difficult thing to forget. Sometimes at a gun show I see those foreign-made weapons. Some of them come from countries we once considered our enemies. Part of me can't help thinking that they must be laughing their heads off at us. They don't have to go to war against us anymore. All they have to do is sell us guns, and we'll do the job for them. And the darnedest part of it is they make a profit.

—Jack Phillips

Blockbuster is right around the corner from school. So I'm in there looking at titles, hoping someone I know will walk in. And who comes in? Emily Kirsch. Like, at first I wasn't even going to talk to her. I went back to looking at titles. But then I look up and there she is, right across the aisle. So we say hi, what's up? You know, the regular BS.

It runs out pretty fast, and there's that moment when

Only a tiny fraction of the guns manufactured in Japan stay in that country. Japan has very strict gun control laws. The majority of the guns manufactured in Japan are shipped to the United States. (_Making a Killing_)

one of you has to come up with something else to say or you're just going to go off in different directions. And I swear I still don't know why I said it, but just joking around, I said, "So, how come you're not at the dance?"

Like she or I would ever go to a school dance.

And that's when she told me about Brendan calling her, and how he wanted to make sure she wouldn't be at the dance. And it just gave me the creepiest feeling. Why would he say that? Since it wasn't like I had anything better to do, I figured I'd walk over to school and take a look.

—Allison Findley

I heard someone scream and then I saw one of them. He was wearing green camouflage clothing and a black ski hat pulled down over his face with the eyes and mouth cut out. At first I thought it was a joke. Guys dressed like commandos and carrying toy guns. But then one of them, I think it was probably Brendan, fired a bunch of shots at the ceiling. It sounded like a pack of firecrackers, but you could hear the bullets pinging and ricocheting off the rafters and air-conditioning ducts. A couple of those big mercury-vapor lights shattered, and glass started to rain down on us. When that happened, most of the crowd dived for the floor.

—Dustin Williams

Do you know what a semiautomatic is? It looks like a machine gun. *Only it's smaller and easier to hide.* It sprays out lots of bullets very quickly. I'm told it has absolutely no use as a hunting weapon and hardly any accuracy, either. So it serves no purpose in target shooting. Then what is it for? Why is it made? What do the companies that make these guns think people are going to do with them?

—Beth Bender

They were running around and yelling and firing at the ceiling. Bullets were ricocheting all over the place. Glass was shattering. It was, like, total mayhem. They told us to lie facedown on the floor with our hands over our head. That made it hard to see. With all the shouting and firing and running, and with the gym semidark because it was a dance, it was hard to tell how many there really were.

I think I knew almost instantly that one of them was Brendan. And that led to the fairly logical conclusion that Gary would be involved too. I took a couple of guesses at who the others might be. I think a lot of us were surprised when we finally realized there weren't any others. It was just Brendan and Gary. Even with the masks you could tell who was who because Brendan was thin and Gary was sort of chubby. You wouldn't have thought only two

---

"The killers [in school shootings] were able to easily acquire high-powered guns, and in many cases, their parents helped the children get them, either directly or through negligence. Guns with rapid-fire capability . . . that can spray a burst of bullets in a matter of seconds, were used in the incidents with the most victims."

—*New York Times*, 6/14/98

of them could make so much noise and gunfire. At first I couldn't understand why they were running and yelling and wearing masks. Now I think it was just to add to the fear factor. Believe me, it worked.

—Dustin Williams

They were yelling at us to get away from the doors. That the doors were booby-trapped. They herded us all into the center of the gym and told us to lie facedown. Mr. Curry tried to get stern and tough, and started to tell Gary to put down the gun. Gary didn't say a word. He just fired off half a dozen quick shots at the ceiling. Those bullets ricocheted around up there. One of them came back down so close to my face I could feel the air move. It sounded like that beach scene in *Saving Private Ryan*.

—Paul Burns

In this school when they get mad, they pull out that walkie-talkie and point it at you. Like it's a stick or a whip or something. Or maybe it's to make sure you know they can get anyone pronto, even the police. It's like an automatic reflex. Mr. Curry pointed his walkie-talkie at Gary and Brendan. And Brendan just shot him.

—Chelsea Baker

The bullet went into the right side of my chest. I thought I was going to die. I thought about my wife, Sara, and my kids. But I was incredibly lucky. It's a story you've heard before. Half an inch this way or that and I wouldn't be here talking to you right now. But the good Lord said it wasn't my time.

—Allen Curry

Of course I was shocked when I heard the news. Everyone around here was. All I could think about was Samantha and Tom Lawlor, and what sweet, kind people they'd been, and about that day four years ago when Samantha had cried in my kitchen. I don't know what happened to Brendan after they left Springfield, but I knew Samantha and Tom well enough to know that nothing they did could have led to anything that extreme. If you've raised children yourself, then you know you can't blame the parents. If a child doesn't want you to know or see something, then you're not going to know or see it.

—Kit Conner

I didn't even know they'd shot Mr. Curry. Most of the kids in the gym didn't know it either. Guns were going off, and people were getting down as fast as they could. Too many things were happening at once.

—Dustin Williams

Airlines are subject to strict federal safety regulations; in 2017 not a single person was killed flying in an American commercial jet. In comparison, 39,773 Americans died in gun deaths the same year. Guns are the only consumer products manufactured in the United States that are not subject to federal health and safety regulation.

The police just couldn't believe that it was an accident that I was at the dance. If they'd spend half as much time trying to help kids with their problems as they did trying to prove that I was an accomplice, we probably wouldn't have these kinds of problems in the first place.

—Allison Findley

I think there might have been an opportunity, right at the beginning, to confront them, challenge them, get them to lay down their weapons. But they had the element of surprise on their side, and they came in firing and making a lot of noise. Once they shot Allen and had the rest of us on our stomachs, they were in control.

—Dick Flanagan

I was one of the first ones they put the plastic ties on. "Aw, look, it's Flach on the floor." [Brendan] pressed the barrel of the gun right against the back of my head. I thought I was dead meat. Then he yanked my hands behind my back and pulled that plastic tie tight. Like a calf-roping contest. Then he kicked me as hard as he could in the ribs, cracked two of them, as it turned out.

—Sam Flach

Several years ago the Winchester-Olin company started selling a new bullet called the Black Talon. It was called the Talon because its tip is divided into six "claws" that unfold as it penetrates flesh. While traveling through the body, this increases the diameter of the bullet nearly three times, causing far more damage than an ordinary bullet.

One of them came over and started putting a tie on my wrists. I asked which one he was, and he said Brendan. I said, "Brendan, come on, it's me, Dustin." He said, "Sorry, dude, it's too late."

—Dustin Williams

They had it planned perfectly. The way they came in firing and yelling. The way they tied up some of the football players and male teachers first. The way they took the walkie-talkies away, and kicked and hurt some of them. By the time I realized how absurd the whole thing was, at least five minutes had passed. I sat up and looked around. There were nearly sixty of us and two of them. They were still tying up some of the bigger boys. I didn't know they'd already shot Allen. I started to get up, and one of them saw me and came running over, yelling at me to get down. I was scared, but I didn't back down. He fired at the ceiling and yelled again for me to lie down. He was still wearing that black mask, but I knew it was Gary. I said, "I'm not lying down, Gary, and I don't think you'll shoot me."

He aimed that gun right at my face and said, "I'd hate to shoot you, Ms. Bender, but I will." I said, "I don't think so." And just like that, he fired. The force of the blast knocked me down, and I was in terrible pain on the left

---

"In Jonesboro and Springfield, the parents of the accused assailants followed the general advice of the National Rifle Association and taught their children, at an early age, how to use guns properly."

—*New York Times*, 6/14/98

side of my head. I didn't know what had happened. I was pretty sure I hadn't been shot. It turned out the bullet missed. But kids all over the gym started screaming and crying. I lay down again. I honestly believe he intentionally missed the first time, but I also think he wouldn't have missed a second time.

—Beth Bender

Several newspapers reported that T. J. Solomon had posters of sports heroes in his room. He was active at his church and attended youth services. One paper reported that he'd led a prayer the day before he shot and wounded six students.

GARY'S SUICIDE NOTE

Dear Mom,

By the time you read this, I'll be gone. I just want you to know that there's nothing you could have done to stop this. I know you always tried your best for me, and if anyone doubts you, just show them this letter.

I don't know if I can really explain why I did this. I guess it's because I know that I'll never be happy. I know that every day of my life will hurt and be a lot more bad than good. It's entirely a matter of, What's the point of living?

I could have just gone and offed myself quietly, but that would have been an even bigger waste. If I go this way, taking the people who made my life miserable with me, then maybe it will send a message. Maybe something will change, and some other miserable kid like me somewhere will get treated better and maybe find a reason to live.

Mom, I could never tell you how unhappy I

was. I knew there was nothing you could do to help, and life has been hard enough on you already. I'm truly, truly sorry that I'm going to put you through so much pain, but I hope that in a year or two you'll get over it. Maybe you could move away and change your name and even have a new kid.

You can start over. I wish I could be there with you, but I'm past the point of no return.

Love forever,
Gary

The Dance

I hid behind the refreshment table. There were three of us there. The other two were preppy, semipopular kids. The kind who hang around on the fringes of the popular clique and get invited in when they need a crowd, like to a game or a dance or a big party. Those two were scared !&*#less. I really think they believed that if Brendan and Gary found them, they'd shoot them.

—Allison Findley

I told them to stop shooting at the ceiling. That a ricocheting bullet could kill someone as easily as an aimed one. One of them instantly fired off another burst. He had to know that the ricochets could have hit him as easily as anyone else. I had to assume he didn't care. I think I'm a reasonably good judge of kids' moods. I can tell when they're putting on an act and bluffing. Believe me, these boys were not putting on an act.

—Dick Flanagan

You want to hear something ironic? The school is about twenty years old, and I recall that there was some argument over the size of the gym when the building designs were first considered. Some people felt it was too large and they were spending too much money on it. But you want to know why I think no one was seriously hurt by a ricocheting bullet? Because that gym is so darn big.

—Allen Curry

I remember wondering why they didn't start shooting kids right away. And I thought, *Oh, no, killing us isn't the point. They have some stupid message they want us to hear first.*

—Deirdre Bunson

Why did they bring flashlights and snacks? Because they weren't planning just to kill those kids. They were going to make them suffer. Just like those kids had made us suffer.

—Allison Findley

I've got pretty broad shoulders, but my arms are short because I'm stocky and not all that tall. Plus they're pretty bulked up from lifting [weights]. It's actually not that easy for me to cross my hands behind my back. They put a tie around my wrists, but it wasn't all that tight. I had some wiggle room.

—Paul Burns

"Bill [Kinkel, Kip's father] . . . hoped buying Kip a legally registered rifle, taking him to a shooting range and seeing that he was taught to use it properly might actually mitigate against the boy's unrelenting fascination with firearms."
—*Rolling Stone*, 9/17/98

Was I surprised when I heard about it? Yeah, for like a second, but not really. Look at it as a form of torture. Day in and day out. Society makes you go to school, and then the society in school tortures you. You realize there's no way out. Everyone has a breaking point. Sooner or later everyone will snap. Maybe if Brendan and Gary hadn't snapped, someone else would have.

—Ryan Clancy

The first bomb went off while they were still tying everyone up. It sounded like it came from outside. Someone asked, "What was that?" and Brendan said it was a warning that they didn't want anyone bothering them. The kids were already so scared they were crying and whimpering. But that bomb just added a whole other dimension of fear. It was one of the many moments that night when I was sure we were all going to die.

—Beth Bender

It was awful. They made us crawl on our stomachs into the center of the gym. The floor was dusty and you had to put your face on it. Then one of them kept an eye on us while the other made some of the girls get up and go sit with their backs to the doors. I wasn't surprised they picked girls. They wouldn't have dared let boys stand up.

—Deirdre Bunson

They were talking about what they were going to do with Sam. And they were talking loud because they wanted everyone to hear. They wanted him to roll over on his back so they could shoot him in the knee. They didn't want to shoot him in the back of the knee, because they weren't sure if that would cripple him or not. They wanted to shoot him in the kneecap. They wanted to make sure he'd be ruined for life.

—Paul Burns

They kept kicking me in the head and the arms and ribs. My hands were tied behind my back, and there was nothing I could do. It hurt worse than anything that ever happened on a football field. They wanted me to roll over so they could shoot me in the knee. I just didn't want to give in. All I could think about was next year's football season. It couldn't end this way. It just couldn't.

—Sam Flach

Try to picture this: fifty or sixty kids lying facedown on that hard gym floor with their hands tied behind their back. Crying, whimpering, blubbering, calling out for mercy, pleading to be let go. It was like these guys were hunters and we were a bunch of seals, and they were trying to decide which ones to slaughter first.

—Dustin Williams

I've been a hunter and gun collector all my life, as well as a dues-paying member of the National Rifle Association for close to thirty years. But when I think that it was my guns that those boys used. That those were my bullets they fired. . . . Sure, you can say that if they hadn't stolen them from me, they would have stolen them from someone else, but they didn't. Those were my guns. And now I have to live with that.

—Jack Phillips

It was hard for me to keep an eye on both of them, but each time I thought they weren't looking, I'd try to work my hands free. I was pretty sure I could get them loose.

—Paul Burns

[The bullet wound] hurt like the dickens. I kept expecting to black out or taste blood in my mouth, but strangely, other than the pain, I felt okay.

—Allen Curry

You couldn't see much. You'd try to lift your head and look around, but after a while your neck muscles would go into spasms and you'd have to put your head back down on that disgusting floor.

—Deirdre Bunson

They shot Sam in both knees. You heard the shots and you heard Sam scream. Some of the teachers started shouting, but they were drowned out by more shots, and

---

"The day of the shootings [in Oregon], the *Eugene Register-Guard* featured a homey little human-interest piece about the wonderful benefits of firearm education."
—*Rolling Stone*, 7/9/98

the sound of the bullets ricocheting all over the ceiling again and more lights shattering. Gary and Brendan yelled at the teachers to shut up. They weren't just out to get the jocks. They were out to get everyone.

—Dustin Williams

I was lying a few feet from Deirdre. She went nuts when they shot Sam in the knees. I really believe she stopped caring about herself. She screamed at Brendan and called him a bastard. She called him a scared little worm and dared him to put down the gun. She went, "Then we'll see how tough you are."

Everyone tried to lift their head to see. I saw Brendan step toward her. Deirdre stopped talking. He knelt down and pressed the barrel of the gun against her cheek. She cried out and jerked away. I think the barrel was hot, and it must have burned her face.

I remember what he said: "Hey, cheerleader, think I give a crap about whether you think I'm tough or not? I already know I'm not tough. You want to know how I know? Because you and your A-hole friends have reminded me every single day since I moved here."

He pressed the barrel of the gun right into the back of her neck. It was really sadistic. Deirdre started to whimper and begged him not to shoot her. Gary came over

---

From 2006 to 2014 an average of 8,300 children a year age seventeen or younger were treated for gunshot wounds in hospital emergency rooms.

and said something about Deirdre having an accident. They both started to laugh. One of the teachers—Mr. Flanagan, I think—yelled at them, and they fired another shot into the gym floor. I felt the vibration against my cheek.

Brendan cursed and said he'd missed. Gary pointed out that he may have missed, but he'd made a nice hole in the wood.

—Paul Burns

After the autopsies, the newspapers said they hadn't been on drugs, but if you ask me, they were acting like totally whacked-out maniacs. They ran around laughing and shooting up the gym floor. You could hear the wood cracking and splintering. I just kept praying they'd run out of ammunition.

—Dustin Williams

It was so scary when they started shooting at the floor. You just felt like they were completely psycho. They stopped because they heard my cell phone ring. My mom made me take it to the dance, and I gave it to Dustin to hold. Brendan went over and took it out of Dustin's pocket.

They told you what he said, didn't they? She asked if I

"'I know some of the guns going out of [my company] end up killing people. . . . But I'm not responsible for that.'"
—Carlos Garcia, whose company, Intratec, manufactured the infamous semiautomatic TEC-9.

was there, and Brendan said yes, but I couldn't come to the phone just then. So my mom asked if I would call her back, and he said he doubted it because I'd probably be dead.

—Chelsea Baker

It was sick. I mean, the way they played with everyone's heads. And that thing with the phone and Chelsea Baker's mom . . . I don't know, it was just completely sick.

—Paul Burns

Sam [Flach] was sobbing and making these horrible, bloodcurdling moans. Someone yelled out that if they didn't get him help, he might bleed to death. And one of those boys smirked and said, "You think?" That's exactly what they wanted. They wanted him to die a slow, wretched death.

—Deirdre Bunson

I heard a metallic clacking and clicking sound. At first I didn't know what it was. I couldn't bend around enough to see. Then I realized it was Brendan and Gary reloading.

—Beth Bender

I heard them reloading and looked over at Beth [Bender]. She gave me a miserable look. We'd both realized the same thing: These boys were well armed. They weren't going to run out of bullets anytime soon.

—Dick Flanagan

Just because someone owns a gun, or likes to hunt or compete in shooting events, does not make him a so-called gun nut. Many people I know own hunting rifles and shotguns, and handguns for self-protection. I can tell you, however, that privately many of us are opposed to semiautomatics. The problem is that once the gun control people get semiautomatics banned, they will go after handguns. And once those are banned, do you know what will happen? Some nut will get ahold of a hunting rifle and kill a bunch of people. The gun control people will use that incident as an excuse to go after hunting rifles.

—Allen Curry

The police got the idea of using the loudspeaker system. We heard a voice come out of nowhere. It really took everyone by surprise, and they handled it very badly. Instead of trying to reason with the boys, they came on very threatening. Laying out what laws they'd broken and what the consequences would be, and how the longer they waited to lay down their weapons, the worse it would be for them.

I remember trying very hard to imagine what those boys were thinking now. And I thought, *Oh, my God, it's too late. They're armed. They're shooting. They've already wounded people. They've taken hostages. They've broken all these laws already. Real laws. Not baby don't-smoke-in-school laws.*

Police estimated that Klebold and Harris fired close to nine hundred rounds during the siege at Columbine.

If they walk out of here alive, they are going to go to jail for a long time. And we all know about that, don't we? What they do to you in there. These poor, crazy boys. Maybe the jocks have tormented them here, but it will be a thousand times worse in jail.

And that's when I had an epiphany. Can't you see why they were doing it? They had no protection. They couldn't get away from the bullies and tormentors. Not here, not in jail, not anywhere. So why not kill them? Why not kill themselves? What difference would it make either way?

—Beth Bender

They started shooting at the ceiling. I assume they were trying to shoot out the speakers. The police shut down the electricity. You can understand why they did it, but when the gym went dark, it just made everything that much worse.

—Dick Flanagan

It went dark, and everyone on the floor just started crying and whimpering even more. It was really pathetic. Brendan and Gary turned on their flashlights. I was scared too. I didn't think they'd shoot me, but I was afraid I might get killed if they blew up the gym or if the police tried to storm in. And as much as I hated Sam Flach, you

---

It is estimated that approximately one million children bring a gun to school each year. Many students who carry guns do so because they are afraid or influenced by peer pressure.

just can't let people suffer like that. So when it went dark, I yelled out to Gary that I was there.

—Allison Findley

As soon as it went dark, kids started inching away from the center of the gym. Those guys would sweep the flashlights over us, and it was like a bunch of giant inchworms crawling around. They yelled at us not to move and went around making sure [the ones who'd moved] went back. That's when I really got to work trying to get my hands free.

—Paul Burns

It was dark. I don't know why, but it reminded me of that scene at the end of *Titanic* where they're all floating in the icy water, just trying to hold on for dear life. They kept sweeping their flashlights around, keeping an eye on everyone. So you'd see those silhouettes of people lying there. Just like in the movie, people were crying out for their loved ones and sobbing. It was really eerie.

—Chelsea Baker

[Later] I told the detectives that the boys appeared to be caught off guard when Allison called out in the dark.

High school students are bringing guns to schools at a much higher rate than is characterized by the federal data, a national survey shows. About 4 percent of high school students say they brought a weapon to school at least once in the past month.

—PBS (Public Broadcasting Service)

Those flashlight beams started swinging around wildly and then focused on the refreshment table. Allison was standing there. She held her hands up and squinted in the lights. When the boys saw her, Brendan seemed amused. He may have even said something like, "Whoa, this is one strange twist." But Gary kept asking her what she was doing there. He was quite upset.

—Beth Bender

Look, who's kidding who? I was scared to death, but when I heard Gary asking Allison why she was there, it scared me even more. You could tell that he expected something really bad to happen, and he didn't want her to be part of it.

—Dustin Williams

When Allison said she thought they should do something to help Sam, the kids became extremely agitated. Up to that point you didn't know whose side she was on.

—Dick Flanagan

It was a madhouse. I mean, twenty people started yelling at Allison at once. I guess they thought she could reason with those guys. Get them to give up or something.

—Paul Burns

"Many times, students will bring a gun to school if they are being bullied, to appear tough to their tormentor."
—Mac Hardy, director of operations, National Association of School Resource Officers

Brendan started yelling at everyone to shut up, and there was a burst of gunfire. It was insane in the dark. You heard gunfire and had no idea who it was. Was it the police? Those guys? Someone else? And then in the middle of it that girl screamed.

—Dustin Williams

I was right next to Robin [Lewis], so when she screamed, I thought they'd shot her. Brendan was yelling at everyone to shut up, but the wailing and crying just tripled. It was beyond nightmarish.

—Beth Bender

In 1995 more than one million guns manufactured outside the United States were imported into this country. By 2017 the number of imported weapons had reached 3.6 million per year.

BRENDAN'S SUICIDE NOTE

To the good people of Middletown:

I hope this gets printed in big, bold letters on the front page of the newspaper, because it's something every single one of you should read. I'm gone now, and you want to know why I took your kids with me?

Here's why. You made my friggin' life miserable. How? By the way you raised your kids to all want to be the same and to hate anyone who dares to be a little different. Oh, no, you're probably thinking, you didn't do that.

You sure did. I've seen you in your cars staring at me and my friends. *Look at those creeps. Look at their clothes and the music they listen to. Why can't they go out for sports or at least root for our team?*

Know what? Not everybody has to do what you A-holes want them to do. Maybe your kids did, but me and my friends chose not to. And you and your kids couldn't deal with that. And so you had to do what stupid, ignorant people always do when they don't understand—you had to attack and torment us.

And you teachers. I thought you taught us that America is supposed to be about freedom. Kids are supposed to be able to be different without the status quo police smashing us over the head and ridiculing us. But that's all you teachers did to me and my friends. Just like everyone else, you tried to make us conform to your narrow-minded expectations of how we were supposed to dress and act.

Well, screw you. Screw all of you. I hope this letter is like a knife in your hearts. You ruined my life. All I've done is pay you back in kind.

Respectfully yours,
Brendan Lawlor

The End

Brendan started to shoot again. From the muzzle flashes I knew he was firing at the ceiling. But in the dark like that a lot of kids couldn't see and didn't know. They just assumed everyone around them was being slaughtered. You don't know what terror really is until you experience it yourself.

—Dustin Williams

Robin [Lewis] screamed because she felt warm liquid seeping into her clothes from the floor and thought it was blood. Everyone knows now it was something else. It's just completely gross.

—Deirdre Bunson

You lose track of how many times you think this is it, you're really going to die now, but that was certainly one of those moments. Brendan was screaming at everyone to shut up. He probably fired that semiautomatic until he'd emptied the whole clip. There were bullets ricocheting all over the place. A couple of kids were grazed. We're incredibly lucky no one was actually hit. It was utter mayhem.

—Allen Curry

It got quiet, and I heard those clicking sounds and realized Brendan was reloading. Then I heard Gary say, "Brendan, we gotta talk." Brendan cursed him out something awful. So now *these* two guys were arguing. I guess it was something in Gary's voice. Everyone who heard it started begging Brendan to listen to him. Of course, that just totally set Brendan off again.

—Chelsea Baker

In a situation like that, you search madly for anything to hope for. When I heard Gary say they had to talk, I thought we had a chance. It wasn't much, but it was all we had. But with all the crying and pleading, Brendan wasn't listening. So I raised my voice and told everyone to quiet down and let the boys talk.

—Beth Bender

First Brendan was screaming at everyone to shut up. Then Ms. Bender said we should be quiet. Then Mr. Flanagan said it too. It was so weird. They were all agreeing with Brendan. For a second I thought they'd gone over to the other side or something.

—Deirdre Bunson

Like any other business, the gun industry must constantly introduce new products to keep buyers interested and enhance profits. People who buy computers look for more memory and faster chip speed. People who buy guns look for increased killing power.

Everyone [on the floor] started whispering to each other to be quiet and let [the boys] talk. In the dark I heard Brendan say he couldn't effing believe it. He just couldn't effing believe it.

—Allison Findley

Gary wanted to talk. Brendan said there was nothing to talk about. They'd chosen their path. So Gary goes, "Things have changed." Brendan started cursing at him and saying nothing had changed. The rest of us just lay there listening to it. Here were these two crazy boys discussing whether we'd live or not. Our lives were totally in their hands.

—Chelsea Baker

I worked my hands free. If there'd just been one [guy with a gun], I think I would have jumped up in the dark and taken him down. But there were two. I thought about grabbing one, getting his gun, and shooting the other, but it seemed awful risky. The truth is I was brought up in a family that was totally against guns and I'd never actually fired one. I wasn't sure I'd know how.

—Paul Burns

Gary said he was still with Brendan all the way, but they had to get Allison out of there. Brendan was completely

---

According to a study of mass shooters conducted by the *Washington Post*, at least 171 mass shooters obtained their weapons legally, while only 59 obtained their weapons illegally.

sarcastic. Like, exactly how did Gary propose to do that? You know, with the doors locked and booby-trapped. Meanwhile, I started to hear this strange sound. Something half whirring, half grinding. I realized it was a drill. Someone was trying to drill into the gym.

—Dustin Williams

They both stopped talking. I heard the drilling sound and knew they were listening too. They started swinging their flashlights over the walls and the basketball nets and the air-conditioning ducts, trying to see where the sound was coming from. I heard a screech of metal and looked up. Of course, it was pitch-black and I couldn't see anything. Those boys were swinging their flashlights around like spotlights at a movie premiere. Then one of the beams fixed on something. It was a black cable wire coming down from the ceiling. Near the end it curved slightly, and something at the very end of it reflected the light from the flashlight beam. I thought, *Well, what do you know? It's a camera.*

—Dick Flanagan

This was unreal. No one's saying anything. Except for the flashlights it's still dark. In the flashlight beam you can

"'We are focusing on dollars more than anything else. . . . For us, a great deal of the motivation is to run a profitable company.'"
—a former president of Smith & Wesson, *Making a Killing*

see this wire thing slowly start to turn in a circle. Like it's looking around to see what the story is.

—Paul Burns

I rolled onto my side a little so I could see what everyone was looking at. It was hard to see the cable, because if the flashlight beam moved just a little, you lost sight of it. Then out of nowhere there's this voice whispering in my ear. It was Paul, and he said he'd gotten his hands free.

—Dustin Williams

I was so glad when I saw that camera come down. So they'd know Brendan and Gary had put us near the doors, and if anyone tried to come in, those doors might explode.

—Chelsea Baker

I have a key ring with a nail clipper on it. It was in the front pocket of my pants. I told Paul to put his hand in my pocket and get it. So Paul put his hand in my pocket and, of course, that's exactly when the lights started to go back on.

—Dustin Williams

You heard that hum, and the lights that weren't shot out started to glow a little. It took a few minutes. I knew Sam was somewhere near me, so I squirmed around until I could see him. He was pale, and his face was a grimace of pain. From the thighs down his pant legs were soaked with blood, and there were dark red puddles on the floor.

I'm not a medical professional, but I sensed it was only a matter of time until he bled to death.

—Beth Bender

[When the lights went on,] Paul's first reaction was to pull his hand out of my pocket. I whispered, "No, get the nail clipper!" He did. Gary and Brendan were so busy looking at the TV camera, they never saw. We were really lucky.

—Dustin Williams

After the lights went back on, they dropped a thinner black wire through the hole. At the end of it was a little, round black thing. It was about the size of one of those microphones you can clip to your collar. Then they turned the gym speakers back on, and this calm voice said, "Brendan? Gary?" Brendan started firing at that tiny microphone. You could tell he didn't like what was happening.

—Deirdre Bunson

It wasn't the same person [on the loudspeaker] as before. This guy was really calm and professional. He told Brendan and Gary that even if they managed to hit the mike and put it out of commission, they'd just send down another one. At first Brendan was fit to be tied, but then he calmed down. I guess he figured out that he was still in control.

—Dustin Williams

Brendan's mom and dad got on the speaker. It was really pitiful. His mom was crying. His dad sounded like he was in agony. They both pleaded with him to stop and give up. They talked about how much they loved him and wanted to help him and how wrong it was to hurt other people and why hadn't he told them how stressed he was? I couldn't see his face because of the mask. But I really wished I could.

—Chelsea Baker

They put on Gary's mom next. She tried to talk, but her voice cracked and she just started to bawl. Then the negotiator guy comes back on and starts talking about how they're not just hurting the people in the gym, they're hurting their families, too. They're destroying their parents' lives. Brendan walked over to Sam Flach, who was still lying there bleeding. He looks up at the little camera and asks if the negotiator guy can see him. The cable turned a little, and the guy said yes. Brendan asked if they could see all the blood seeping out of Sam's knees, and the negotiator said yes. Brendan knelt down and put the barrel of his gun right next to Sam's ear and said that if they didn't remove that camera and mike right now, he would put a bullet in Sam's head. The next thing we knew, the camera and microphone started to rise back up to the ceiling.

—Allison Findley

Paul had the nail clippers, but with the lights on, Brendan and Gary could see us. I was praying to God as hard as I could that the lights would go off again.

—Dustin Williams

I'm not sure I believe in miracles, but ever since that night, I definitely believe in angels. Only you never know who they might be or what form they might take. If Allison Findley could be an angel, anyone could.

—Dick Flanagan

I heard a really horrible groan. Allison was kneeling over Sam, and at first I thought she was torturing him or something. But she'd taken off her belt and put it around one of Sam's thighs and was tightening it like a tourniquet. Brendan yelled at her to get away from Sam. Allison said no without even looking at him. Brendan came over and said he'd kill her if she didn't leave Sam alone. Allison looked up at him and said, "Know what, Brendan? I know you don't care about living. Well, neither do I. Go ahead and kill me." Maybe she knew Brendan wouldn't shoot her. Maybe she truly didn't care.

—Chelsea Baker

Paul and I weren't that far from Sam. Allison used her belt to try and stop the bleeding in one of his legs, and then she started to look around for another belt. So naturally she looked at guys. Paul had his hands behind him, like he was pretending they were still tied. He had the nail clipper in his fist. Allison walked over to us and

---

"'The big thing about firearms is that they do give the weak a way to defend themselves against the strong.'"
—William Ruger Sr., president of Ruger, a manufacturer of semiautomatic weapons, *Making a Killing*

looked down at him. My heart was beating so hard I thought I was going to puke.

—Dustin Williams

Brendan and Gary were standing shoulder to shoulder, arguing. One faced one way, the other faced the other way. So they were each watching 180 degrees of the room. I assumed they were fighting about Allison. At first I didn't quite grasp it. What was the big deal? Why did they care if she stayed? Just because she was there didn't necessarily mean she'd have to come to harm, did it? Not unless they were planning to kill everyone . . . including themselves.

—Beth Bender

Allison bent over Paul. I saw her look down at him, then kind of blink and straighten up. I thought, *This is it. Good-bye, world. I hope Heaven's exactly the same way they pictured it in that* South Park *movie.*

—Dustin Williams

It wasn't really an argument. It was Brendan yelling at Gary about what they'd agreed on and how hard they'd worked, and how if they didn't do this, nothing would ever change. And Gary looking like he had a headache, closing his eyes and pressing his fingers against his temple and saying over and over again, "I know, I know, I know." And I kept thinking, what had they worked so hard for? And you knew it was this. The planning and the booby-trapping and the bombs, and I couldn't help imagining the effort that must have gone into it. What an enormous force it must have been that twisted these boys' minds to the point that they would work so hard to do this.

—Beth Bender

[Allison] was standing right over me. I started saying good-bye to everyone. I mean, in my head. I guess I closed my eyes, because when I opened them Allison was still staring at me.

—Paul Burns

The Lord says we should do unto others as we would have them do unto us. It's not very complicated.

—Chelsea Baker

[Allison] walked away. For a second I thought she was going to tell Brendan and Gary. But she knelt down next to Joey Graves and told him she was going to undo his belt. Can you believe Joey? He actually said he'd always dreamed of that. Allison said, "Don't be an A-hole."

—Paul Burns

"The ultimate fact is that the gun industry is simply a business. . . . The people who make, import and sell guns . . . are businessmen. They want to make money, and as much of it as possible."

—Making a Killing

The way I heard it, she took Joey's belt and went over to Sam and did the same thing she'd done to his other leg. You know, the doctor said if she hadn't done that, he probably would have bled to death. The thing is, can you picture that? Allison Findley saving Sam Flach's life?

—Ryan Clancy

Brendan went ballistic on Gary. He yanked off his mask and threw it on the floor. And Gary, I don't know, he just shut down. He walked over to the wall, sat down, and buried his head in his arms. Now Brendan's storming around, yelling great, just effing great! Neither of them was paying attention to anything. Dustin nudged me with his foot, and I rolled around and clipped the tie holding his hands.

—Paul Burns

It sounded like a firecracker. Everyone was looking around like, *What was that?* Allison screamed out Gary's name. He was lying on his side. It was horrible.

—Chelsea Baker

I wanted more guys, but when Gary shot himself, I didn't know what was going to happen next. Allison went running to Gary. Brendan followed her, but he was walking.

"Time and time again, the gun industry has injected into the civilian market new guns that are specifically designed to be better at killing."

—*Making a Killing*

He had his back to us. We do up-downs in football. That's where we drop to our stomach, then jump back up. The coaches are always on me because I'm not the fastest to get up, but I was then.

I knew Brendan was going to hear me coming. I was just hoping he wouldn't have time to turn around, aim, and fire.

—Dustin Williams

It didn't seem real. That little popping noise, and then Gary slumped over and the blood started to run out of his head. His arms and legs started jerking. It was just so gross. I kept thinking, *No way. This is a dream. It's a movie.*

—Deirdre Bunson

[Brendan] heard my footsteps and started to turn with the gun, but I tackled him as hard as I could and slammed him down against the gym floor. That #$*%ing gun slid away, and I held Brendan down. He struggled and cursed a lot, but that was it.

—Dustin Williams

Dustin Williams is a hero. There's no doubt about that.

—Allen Curry

They say Dustin's a hero, but I don't believe he was trying to be one. I think he was only doing what he knew had to

---

More American children are killed by firearms than by all natural causes combined.

be done. Something bad was going on, and he had to stop it. It's what a moral human being is supposed to do.

—Chelsea Baker

We all saw what happened. Suddenly every kid was screaming for Paul to free them. Can you blame them? We all wanted to get out of there. That's when I remembered the doors were booby-trapped.

—Beth Bender

It was complete hysteria. Paul was going around with those clippers, cutting the ties as fast as he could. Someone else found a pair of nail clippers, and one of the boys had a penknife. The kids were crying and shrieking to be freed next. That little eye-in-the-sky camera must have been watching the whole time, because the loudspeaker started blaring. But it was lost in the din. Someone started shouting to stay away from the doors, but not everyone was paying attention.

—Dick Flanagan

I was holding Brendan down. He was cursing and crying and squirming. I'm not going to name names, but someone grabbed me from behind and yanked me off. At least six other guys were on him in no time.

—Dustin Williams

I tried to get up, but I couldn't. The slightest movement

and the pain was overwhelming. It's not like the movies. At least it wasn't for me. You don't get hit and keep going. You get shot and you go down and stay there.

—Allen Curry

At that point I wasn't thinking about Brendan. I was thinking about the kids who were heading for the doors. They were chained shut, but we knew they were booby-trapped. We had to make sure those kids stayed away from the doors. We had no idea how much or how little it might take to make one blow.

—Dick Flanagan

Dustin was holding Brendan. I don't think Brendan was going to escape. Those boys got free, and the first thing on their minds was to get Brendan. I still don't understand what they were thinking.

—Chelsea Baker

You had four exits. You ran to one, and if there was already someone there trying to keep the kids from pulling on the doors, you ran to the next [set of doors] and tried to stop those kids. Some of them understood, but some of them were panicked and irrational. To be honest, I wasn't really aware of what else was going on.

—Dick Flanagan

They wanted to kill him. The way they were stomping on

his head, it was sickening. He wasn't even conscious. Just limp like a doll.

—Dustin Williams

I tried to stop them. I was the only one. One of them cursed me out and pushed me away. Then I went to get Ms. Bender. She was telling kids to stay away from the doors. I told her they were killing Brendan. She told me to keep everyone away from the doors and ran over there.

—Allison Findley

What Brendan and Gary did was terribly, horribly, inexcusably wrong. I have no interest in defending them. But deep in my heart there's a little piece of me that at least understands what might have driven them to such a horrendous, evil undertaking. But what those boys did was equally inexcusable and evil.

—Beth Bender

I didn't try to stop [the boys beating Brendan]. I guess at that point I was just so wiped out and stressed that I didn't care. I know those guys have to be punished. The police have already told my parents I'll have to testify about what I saw. This may sound terrible, but I still

---

In 1997, after a man armed with handguns killed sixteen children and a teacher at Dunblane Primary School in Scotland, Britain banned all handguns.

wonder, if I had to do it again, would I try to stop them next time? And I don't know what the answer is.

—Dustin Williams

Everyone is convinced that Brendan and Gary would have let Sam die, and would have killed many more. Maybe they're right. Maybe not. The fact is the only person Gary killed was himself. And Brendan didn't kill anyone. I know he shot Sam and Mr. Curry, but maybe [Brendan and Gary] would have changed their minds and let everyone live. Maybe they would have let Sam bleed a little longer and then gotten him help. No one will ever know. But this much I do know: The only people I saw really try to kill anyone that night were those boys. They tried to kill Brendan with their bare hands. And I am absolutely convinced that if it hadn't been for Ms. Bender, they would have.

—Allison Findley

I speak to Mrs. Lawlor about once a week. Brendan is still in a coma. The doctors say his brain damage is irreversible. The courts will have to decide whether to disconnect his life support. Apparently there's a group of people somewhere

---

"After thirty-five people were killed by a gunman with an array of assault weapons . . . in 1996, Australia banned all automatic and semiautomatic weapons and pump-action shotguns, paid their owners a fair price, and destroyed the lot."

—Making a Killing

who are against it. Whoever they are, they certainly don't know the Lawlors or anyone else around here. Sometimes I wonder what has happened to the world. How we got to a place where mercy seems so hard to come by.

—Beth Bender

You want to know what it was? Pure evil, plain and simple. How else do you explain a boy being as nice and polite as Brendan Lawlor and then doing what he did?

—Jack Phillips

I've been awarded a partial scholarship to an Ivy League college back east. Back where all the "liberal gun control" people live. I bet half the newspaper editors who wrote editorials attacking our school went to that kind of college. I had good grades and boards, but I know kids, even African American kids like me, who had better grades and boards and didn't get into one of those schools. Know why I got in? Because I made second-team all-state linebacker. One of those Ivy League teams back east needed a linebacker. Kind of ironic, huh?

—Dustin Williams

My pastor says I have to try and forgive them for what they did to me. Meanwhile I'm still on crutches with two knees that'll never be any good again. Why? Did I do anything that a thousand other guys at a thousand other schools haven't done? Sorry, folks, I'm not forgiving them. Ever.

—Sam Flach

The memory of what happened surrounds me like a cloak of pain. A hundred questions buzz around my head: How did it happen? When did it go from a fantasy to an actual plan? I know I'll never understand what happened in Brendan's mind. But I thought I knew Gary better. What pushed him over the line? How did he get to the point where he just didn't care? What really scares me is when I think about how close I came to that point myself.

—from Allison Findley's journal

A schoolteacher's job is to teach, not to raise children. As far as raising children, I raised my three just fine. They are all good, moral young adults, and two of them own guns, which they use for target shooting and hunting. If you're looking for answers, you're not going to find them in school. Many people around here believe that, at least in this case, the parents were pretty blameless. I'll be honest with you. I don't know what to think about that. And I don't have any answers.

—Dick Flanagan

I've heard the argument that it's okay to give guns to kids as long as you make sure they're trained on how to

---

"'We'll never understand why this tragedy happened, or what we might have done to prevent it. . . . We did not see anger or hatred in Dylan until the last moments of his life, when we watched in helpless horror with the rest of the world.'"
—Dylan Klebold's parents, *New York Times*, 6/29/99

use them safely. I have to disagree. These are children, and they can be extremely emotional and impulsive and not always completely in touch with reality. The statistics show that guns are now the number one killer of young people in this country. You can train a young man all you want, but if he's just been dumped by his girlfriend, or picked on by someone much bigger and stronger than him . . . well, I'm just not convinced that all the safety training in the world is going to stop him from grabbing that gun and doing what he thinks he has to do.

—Beth Bender

The community has made it clear that they want metal detectors and security guards in school. They want backpacks banned as well. I think it's a shame that we have to resort to these measures, but if that's what the community wants, I'm prepared to comply.

—Allen Curry

There was an article in the newspaper recently about the NRA paying for programs that promote hunting and gun use among children. I have nothing against hunting. My dad hunted, and some of my fondest memories are of sitting around the dinner table eating venison and hearing his hunting stories. But personally, I think hunting is something parents can teach their children about, just like my father learned from his father. I don't understand why a big national organization feels it must spend all this money to make sure children learn about guns.

—Kit Conner

Want to know what a trigger lock is? It's something you take off a gun and throw away.

—Jack Phillips

I'm not sure what it will take to change. Everyone knows that guns and violence are deeply ingrained in our culture. You've got about as much chance of getting people to give up their guns as you do getting them to give up driving or drinking beer at baseball games. Innocent victims die because of guns, but they also die because of car accidents, acts of terrorism, fires, and food poisoning. We find the idea of kids being killed in school especially repugnant because we send our children there expecting them to be safe. But it appears that no place is safe anymore.

—F. Douglas Ellin

I sincerely believe that this tragedy didn't have to happen. Maybe Gary and Brendan were different from other kids, but they still should have been accepted as people. Maybe there should be a mandatory course in school that teaches kids to respect one another no matter what. I think that would be a lot more helpful than geometry.

—Emily Kirsch

I read in the newspaper that the kind of guns they had are pretty much the same thing the army uses. They're not made for hunting or target practice. They're just made to kill people. Why in the world are stores allowed to sell them?

—Chelsea Baker

I used to drive through towns and see signs proclaiming, "Drug-Free Zone." Now the signs say, "Gun-Free Zone." But by the time they're thinking about guns, it's too late. The signs should read, "Teasing/Bullying–Free Zone." My son was different, and he was made to pay for that every day of his short life. Perhaps if we spent as much time teaching tolerance as we do teaching athletics, my son would be alive today.

—Cynthia Searle

Even now when I go to school, I know I'm being watched. Ryan and I leave little pieces of paper wedged in the bottom of our locker doors, and about once a week they're gone. We walk down the hall, and teachers stop talking. Nothing's changed. In fact, in some ways it's gotten worse. If you act different or dress different, you're automatically suspect.

—Allison Findley

A program for resolving conflicts creatively was tested in New York City public elementary schools. It was found that students in the program tended to be less hostile and were more likely to choose verbal rather than physical strategies to resolve conflicts.

In the wild, animals pick on the weaker members of the pack. This is done partly to establish a pecking order and partly to protect the pack against weakness. It is no different with children. Teasing, bullying, fighting—these are how children establish their pecking order. It is, unfortunately, natural for children to do this. And it is the responsibility of adults to supervise and stop this behavior. One thing that is wrong with our schools is that we are permitting too much of the former and not enough of the latter.

—F. Douglas Ellin

I think about the stuff we did—fooling around with bombs and guns, drinking and driving—things that could really kill us. But we didn't know. I swear it was like we were living in some make-believe world. I truly believe that if Gary and Brendan could come back now and see what they did—to themselves and their parents and everyone else—they wouldn't have done it. No one would.

—Ryan Clancy

"'We have a little moneymaking machine here. All we have to do is keep introducing the correct new products. . . . We operate on a philosophy that you have to have new stuff, and you have to have it annually.'"
—William Ruger Sr., president of Ruger, a gun company whose semiautomatic handguns were used by Colin Ferguson to kill six and wound nineteen on a Long Island Railroad train, and by Michael Carneal to kill three and wound five in Paducah, Kentucky, *Making a Killing*

We live in a culture of brutality. People seem to think that it's perfectly acceptable to be violent. Look at wrestling on TV. Even when it's fake, we love the savageness of it. Maybe that's the norm outside of school, but I am just plain sorry—when it happens in school, you cannot simply walk away from it and say boys will be boys. It must be stopped.

—Beth Bender

"'It's not my fault. It really isn't.'"
—the president of a major gun manufacturer,
when asked about the gun industry's responsibility
for firearms violence, Making a Killing

Postscript

I have spent hundreds of hours interviewing, listening, and reading. Even after all that, I still don't know what went on in Gary's mind. Didn't he know there were alternatives? He could have transferred to another school or even dropped out altogether. How did he get to the point where he believed guns and bombs were the only way to solve his problems?

I stand outside Middletown High, the school I graduated from just three years ago, and I know I'm a changed person. We all are. In Middletown, in our state, in this country. Around the world. Can anything good come from this? Is any lesson worth this cost? Two lives destroyed at Middletown High School. At other schools, dozens more lives lost. Kids who had as much right to live as any of us, gone. Robbed in moments of absolute insanity.

What I do know is that from now on I will pay attention more carefully—not just to the words and what they mean, but to whom they're coming from. I think we are too often fooled by the outward sophistication of

---

After a school shooting in Canada, the Canadian government spent $1 million to expand programs to combat bullying in schools and to help students before they get into trouble.

teenagers. We forget that they are still children, and that they are impressionable and impulsive and likely to follow the example of adults. If the teachers and administrators at a school are intolerant of differences between students, then some of the students are likely to follow their lead.

And if I ever decide to have children, I will make sure they go to a school where civility is taught and where differences between people are embraced, not ridiculed. In this country we have raised consciousness about drunk driving, smoking, and drug use. We can do the same with respecting others.

And the guns. There are millions of people in this country who own hunting and target weapons and use them responsibly. I don't think hunting weapons should be outlawed, but I do believe it is time for compromise. Most semiautomatic weapons serve no purpose other than to kill people. They should be outlawed. In this time of budget surpluses, the government should pay a fair price for the semiautomatics that already exist and destroy them. Handguns should be in the hands of law enforcement agencies. The sale and importation of ammunition should be strictly regulated.

"'What made the difference [in my vote]? . . . Twelve dead children, one dead adult, twenty-four injured kids, and a community that has had its heart broken. . . .'"
—Colorado Republican Congressman Tom Tancredo, who accepted a campaign donation from the NRA but voted for gun control after seeing what happened at Columbine High School. Congressman Tancredo lives in Littleton, Colorado. *New York Times*, 6/21/99

Gary Searle was my stepbrother. He wasn't a monster, just a boy who thought he'd run out of options. He was part of my life. I loved him; I still do. It is too late to help him, but we all know others like him. I will try to help them. And maybe, after reading this story, you will too.

—Denise Shipley

While This Book Was Being Written

7/29/1999—Mark O. Barton kills nine and wounds twelve in an office in Atlanta. He uses two handguns.

8/10/1999—Buford O. Furrow Jr. kills a postal worker with a Glock handgun and uses an Uzi submachine gun to wound four children and one adult at the North Valley Jewish Community Center in Los Angeles.

9/15/1999—Larry Gene Ashbrook kills seven people (including four teens) in church. He uses a 9 mm semiautomatic Ruger pistol.

10/4/1999—A New York City school principal is wounded by a student carrying a gun.

10/11/1999—Under the weight of twenty-eight lawsuits filed by various cities and counties, the Colt Manufacturing Company announces plans to stop selling handguns to the public. Sales in the future will be limited to the military and law enforcement agencies.

10/13/1999—New Jersey becomes the fourth state to prohibit the sale of any new handgun unless it is accompanied by a trigger lock.

10/29/1999—South High School in Cleveland is closed and the homecoming dance canceled after officials discover an alleged plan by four students to shoot others. The school was searched and no guns or other weapons were found, prompting some to wonder how serious the plan was. Other students reported that the four were among a group of kids who were considered outcasts and were often picked on.

11/1/1999—A high school in Redmond, Washington, is closed by the administration after threats are made on the Internet to kill everyone at school.

11/2/1999—Byran Uyesugi, age forty, described as a gun enthusiast who owned close to twenty weapons, shoots and kills seven people in an office in Honolulu.

11/19/1999—A thirteen-year-old Denver boy is wounded when a bomb goes off in his bedroom. Authorities say that the boy had been involved in a fight at school several days before.

11/19/1999—Victor Cordova, thirteen, critically wounds a thirteen-year-old classmate in the lobby of their New Mexico middle school. Cordova uses a handgun in the attack.

12/6/1999—In Fort Gibson, Oklahoma, a thirteen-year-old boy wounds four classmates. He uses his father's semi-automatic handgun.

12/8/1999—In Veghel, Netherlands, in the first school shooting in the country's history, a seventeen-year-old boy wounds four students and a teacher with a handgun.

12/21/1999—In Oswego, Kansas, five teens are charged with conspiracy to commit murder after their plot to kill students, teachers, and administrators is discovered. Police confiscate close to forty weapons from their homes.

12/30/1999—In Tampa, Florida, a man armed with a semi-automatic handgun kills five and wounds three in the lobby and pool area of a Radisson hotel.

2/29/2000—In Mount Morris Township, Michigan, six-year-old Kayla Rolland is shot to death in her first-grade classroom by a six-year-old classmate who used a handgun he had found at home.

3/17/2000—Reacting to lawsuits, Smith & Wesson, the country's biggest handgun manufacturer, agrees to add trigger locks to each new handgun it sells, and to restrictions designed to make it more difficult for criminals to purchase handguns.

5/11/2000—In Prairie Grove, Arkansas, a seventh-grade student and a police officer are both wounded from firing at each other after the student was reported walking down a country road with a shotgun. According to police reports, the student had obtained the gun from his home and was returning to school after he was angered by something the principal had said to him.

5/14/2000—Hundreds of thousands of mothers and their families gather in front of the Capitol in Washington, D.C., for the Million Mom March. The event was organized for "common sense" gun control legislation. In addition to licensing and registration, the marchers called for built-in locks on all guns and a ban on military-style assault rifles.

A Partial List of Mass Shootings

12/30/1974—*Olean, New York*

Anthony Barbaro kills three and wounds nine at his high school.

5/28/1975—*Centennial Secondary School, Brampton, Ontario, Canada*

Sixteen-year-old Michael Slobodian kills one teacher and one student, and wounds thirteen others, then commits suicide.

10/19/1978—*Sturgeon Creek Regional Secondary School, Winnipeg, Manitoba, Canada*

A seventeen-year-old student kills a sixteen-year-old student.

1/29/1979—*San Diego, California*

Sixteen-year-old Brenda Spencer uses a rifle given to her as a birthday present to kill two and wound nine at an elementary school near her home.

7/18/1984—*McDonald's, San Ysidro, California*

Forty-one-year-old James Huberty, armed with a semiautomatic pistol, an Uzi carbine, and a shotgun, kills twenty-one people and wounds an additional nineteen before being killed by police.

12/10/1985—*Portland Junior High School, Portland, Connecticut*
A thirteen-year-old student opens fire at a junior high school, killing a janitor and wounding two others. He uses a TEC-9 semiautomatic handgun.

12/16/1988—*Atlantic Shores Christian School, Virginia Beach, Virginia*
Sixteen-year-old Nicholas Elliot kills a teacher and a student with a Cobray semiautomatic handgun with multiple thirty-two-round clips.

1/5/1993—*Brentwood High School, Brentwood, New York*
Shooting erupts during a high school basketball game. One student is wounded.

1/18/1993—*East Carter High School, Grayson, Kentucky*
Seventeen-year-old Scott Pennington kills a teacher and a custodian. He uses a handgun.

2/1/1993—*Amityville, New York*
Seventeen-year-old Shem McCoy kills one student and wounds another. He uses a nine-shot .22-caliber semiautomatic handgun.

10/21/1994—*Brockton High School, Toronto, Ontario, Canada*
A student allegedly unhappy with his grades shoots two guidance counselors.

10/12/1995—*Blackville, South Carolina*
A sixteen-year-old kills one teacher and wounds another, then kills himself.

10/23/1995—*Redlands, California*
A thirteen-year-old kills one student and wounds another.

11/15/1995—*Richland High School, Lynnville, Tennessee*
Seventeen-year-old Jamie Rouse opens fire with a rifle in a crowded school hallway. He kills one student and one teacher, and wounds one teacher.

2/2/1996—*Frontier Junior High School, Moses Lake, Washington*
Fourteen-year-old honor student Barry Loukaitis kills two students and one teacher, using two guns he took from an unlocked cabinet at home and a .25-caliber semi-automatic pistol from the family car.

2/28/1996—*St. Louis, Missouri*
A teenager is shot to death on a school bus and the driver is wounded. The assailant uses a .38-caliber semiautomatic handgun.

2/19/1997—*Bethel, Alaska*
Sixteen-year-old Evan Ramsey kills two students and wounds two others with a 12-gauge shotgun left unlocked in his home.

10/1/1997—*Pearl High School, Pearl, Mississippi*
Sixteen-year-old Luke Woodham kills his mother, then goes to school and kills two students and wounds seven others.

12/1/1997—*Heath High School, Paducah, Kentucky*
Fourteen-year-old Michael Carneal opens fire on an early-morning prayer circle, killing three girls and wounding five other students. He uses a .22-caliber Ruger semiautomatic handgun he had taken, along with two shotguns and two rifles, from a neighbor's house. He carries five hundred rounds of ammunition in his backpack.

12/15/1997—*Stamps High School, Stamps Arkansas*
Fourteen-year-old Joseph Todd kills two students.

3/24/1998—*Westside Middle School, Jonesboro, Arkansas*
Eleven-year-old Andrew Golden and thirteen-year-old Mitchell Johnson kill four students and one teacher, and wound ten others. They arm themselves with three handguns taken from Golden's parents' house, and four handguns and three rifles taken from Golden's grandfather's home, where they were left unlocked.

4/24/1998—*J. W. Parker Middle School, Edinboro, Pennsylvania*
Fourteen-year-old Andrew Jerome Wurst shoots and kills a science teacher and wounds two students and another teacher at an eighth-grade graduation dance. He uses a .25-caliber handgun registered to his father.

5/19/1998—*Lincoln County High School, Fayetteville, Tennessee*
Jacob Davis, an eighteen-year-old honor student, kills a student allegedly dating his ex-girlfriend.

5/21/1998—*Thurston High School, Springfield, Oregon*
Fifteen-year-old Kipland Kinkel kills his parents and then goes to school and kills two students and wounds twenty-two others. He uses a .22-caliber semiautomatic Ruger handgun, a 9 mm Glock handgun, and a Ruger semiautomatic rifle with a fifty-round clip. The rifle was purchased for him by his parents. The handguns were his father's.

6/15/1998—*Armstrong High School, Richmond, Virginia*
Fourteen-year-old student Quinshawn Booker shoots and wounds a basketball coach and a volunteer aide. Another student was the intended victim. He uses a .32-caliber Llama semiautomatic handgun.

4/20/1999—*Columbine High School, Littleton, Colorado*
Eighteen-year-old Eric Harris and seventeen-year-old Dylan Klebold kill twelve students and one teacher and wound twenty-three others, then kill themselves. They use a TEC-9 semiautomatic handgun, a 9 mm Hi-Point semiautomatic carbine rifle, and two sawed-off shotguns.

4/28/1999—*W. R. Myers High School, Taber, Alberta, Canada*
A fourteen-year-old student kills one student and wounds a second. He uses a .22-caliber rifle.

5/20/1999—*Heritage High School, Conyers, Georgia*
Fifteen-year-old T. J. Solomon wounds six students. He uses a .22-caliber rifle and a .357-caliber handgun. Both had to be sneaked past a school security officer and two other security staffers.

3/5/2001—*Santana High School, Santee, California*
Fifteen-year-old Charles Andrew Williams kills two students and wounds thirteen others. He uses his father's .22-caliber revolver.

4/26/2002—*Gutenberg Gymnasium, Erfurt, Germany*
Nineteen-year-old Robert Steinhäuser uses a shotgun and semiautomatic pistol to kill twelve teachers, an administrator, two students, and a police officer before committing suicide.

3/21/2005—*Red Lake Senior High School, Red Lake, Minnesota*
After killing his grandfather and grandfather's companion at their home with his grandfather's semiautomatic pistols, sixteen-year-old Jeffrey Weise kills five students, one teacher, and one security guard, and wounds seven others before committing suicide.

10/2/2006—*West Nickel Mines School, Nickel Mines, Pennsylvania*
Thirty-two-year-old Charles Carl Roberts IV kills five girls and wounds five others before killing himself. He is armed with a semiautomatic handgun, a 12-gauge shotgun, and a rifle, and about 600 rounds of ammunition.

4/16/2007—*Virginia Tech, Blacksburg, Virginia*
Twenty-three-year-old Seung-Hui Cho kills thirty-two students and faculty members, and wounds another seventeen, before committing suicide. He uses two semiautomatic pistols.

11/7/2007—*Jokela High School, Tuusula, Finland*
Eighteen-year-old Pekka-Eric Auvinen uses a semiautomatic pistol to kill six students, the school principal, and school nurse before committing suicide.

2/14/2008—*Northern Illinois University, DeKalb, Illinois*
Twenty-seven-year-old Steven Kazmierczak kills five and injures twenty-one people with a shotgun. He then commits suicide.

9/23/2008—*Kauhajoki Vocational School, Kauhajoki, Finland*
Twenty-two-year-old Matti Juhani Saari kills nine students and a staff member and injures eleven with a semiautomatic pistol and homemade Molotov cocktails. Saari commits suicide.

3/11/2009—*Albertville Secondary School, Winnenden, Germany*
Seventeen-year-old Tim Kretschmer uses a semiautomatic pistol to kill nine students and two teachers, and injures seven others. He escapes and kills 3 more people before committing suicide.

4/30/2009—*Azerbaijan State Oil Academy, Baku, Azerbaijan*
Armed with a semiautomatic pistol, twenty-nine-year-old Farda Gadirov kills twelve people and wounds thirteen, then commits suicide.

4/7/2011—*Rio de Janeiro, Brazil*
Twenty-three-year-old Willington Manezes de Oliveira kills sixteen children and wounds twelve before committing suicide. He uses two handguns.

7/22/2011—*Olso and Utoya, Norway*
After using a car bomb to kill eight people and severely wound twelve more in Olso, thirty-two-year-old Anders Breivik, armed with two semiautomatic weapons, travels to the island of Utoya, where he kills sixty-nine young people and wounds dozens more. Breivik was captured by police, convicted, and imprisoned.

2/27/2012—*Chardon High School, Chardon, Ohio*
Seventeen-year-old Thomas Lane kills three students and wounds three with a handgun.

4/2/2012—*Oikos University, Oakland, California*
Forty-three-year-old One L. Goh kills seven students and wounds three others with a handgun.

12/14/2012—*Sandy Hook Elementary School, Newtown, Connecticut*
After killing his mother at home, twenty-year-old Adam Lanza kills twenty-six people, including twenty first-grade children aged six and seven. He then commits suicide. He uses his mother's weapons—a 12-gauge semiautomatic shotgun, a semiautomatic rifle, and two semiautomatic handguns.

10/24/2014—*Marysville Pilchuck High School, Marysville, Washington*
Armed with a semiautomatic handgun, fifteen-year-old Jaylen Fryberg kills four students and wounds a fifth before committing suicide.

10/1/2015—*Umpqua Community College, Roseburg, Oregon*
Armed with five handguns and a rifle, twenty-six-year-old Christopher Harper-Mercer kills eight students and one teacher and injures nine others. Mercer then commits suicide.

1/22/2016—*La Loche, Community School, La Loche, Canada*
A seventeen-year-old (name not released) kills two brothers at their home and two teachers. Seven others at the school are wounded.

6/12/2016—*Pulse Nightclub, Orlando, Florida*
Twenty-nine-year-old Omar Mateen, armed with a semi-automatic rifle and a 9-millimeter semiautomatic pistol, kills forty-nine people and wounds fifty-three others. Orlando Police Department officers shoot and kill Mateen after a three-hour standoff.

10/1/2017—*Mandalay Bay Resort, Las Vegas, Nevada*
Sixty-four-year-old Stephen Paddock, armed with twenty-three firearms, a large quantity of ammunition, and numerous high-capacity magazines capable of holding up to a hundred rounds apiece kills fifty-eight people and wounds 527. Fourteen of the firearms are .223-caliber AR-15-type semiautomatic rifles. Paddock fires more than eleven hundred rounds of ammunition from his suite on the thirty-second floor of the resort and casino. He is

later found dead in his room from a self-inflicted gunshot wound. His motive remains undetermined.

11/5/2017—*First Baptist Church, Sutherland Springs, Texas*
Twenty-six-year-old Devin Patrick Kelley, armed with a semiautomatic rifle, kills twenty-six people (including an unborn baby) and wounds twenty others. Kelley later dies from a self-inflicted gunshot wound.

12/7/2017—*Aztec, New Mexico*
Twenty-one-year-old William Atchison, armed with a handgun, kills two students at his former high school before he takes his own life. He was investigated in 2016 by the FBI because he had asked in an online forum "where to find cheap assault rifles for a mass shooting."

1/23/2018—*Marshall County High School, Benton, Kentucky*
Fifteen-year-old Gabriel Ross Parker is accused of using a handgun to shoot sixteen people. Two students are killed and fourteen are wounded.

2/14/2018—*Marjory Stoneman Douglas High School, Parkland, Florida*
Nineteen-year-old former student Nikolas Cruz is accused of killing seventeen students and staff members with a semiautomatic rifle, and wounding seventeen more. He is awaiting trial.

5/18/2018—*Santa Fe Hgh School, Santa Fe, Texas*
Seventeen-year-old Dimitrios Pagourtzis is accused of using a shotgun and handgun to kill ten and wound thirteen. Police also discover multiple improvised explosive devices (typically referred to as IEDs): The list includes a pressure cooker, which can be modified into an

IED; Molotov cocktails; pipe bombs; propane tanks; and other homemade explosives around the school and parking lot. He is awaiting trial.

10/17/2018—*Kerch Polytechnic College, Kerch, Crimea*
Eighteen-year-old Vladislav Roslyakov uses a shotgun to kill seventeen students and wound forty more people during a fifteen-minute rampage through the campus.

10/27/2018—*Tree of Life Synagogue, Pittsburgh, Pennsylvania*
Forty-six-year-old Robert Gregory Bowers is accused of using a semiautomatic rifle and three semiautomatic pistols to kill eleven and injure six. After his arrest, Bowers is charged with forty-four federal crimes. He is awaiting trial.

11/7/2018—*Borderline Bar and Grill, Thousand Oaks, California*
Twenty-eight-year-old Ian David Long, armed with a semiautomatic pistol, kills twelve and injures eighteen. Long later dies of a self-inflicted gunshot wound.

3/13/2019—*Suzano, Brazil*
Seventeen-year-old Guilherme Taucci Monteiro and twenty-five-year-old Luiz Henrique de Castro, both former students at the Professor Raul Brasil State School, kill eight students and school employees.

4/30/2019—*University of North Carolina, Charlotte, North Carolina*
Twenty-two-year-old former student Trystan Terrell uses a handgun to kill two and wound four. Terrell was sentenced to life in prison without the possibility of parole.

5/31/2019—*Virginia Beach, Virginia*
Forty-year-old DeWayne Antonio Craddock, armed with two semiautomatic pistols, kills twelve people and wounds

four others in a municipal building. Craddock is later shot dead by police officers responding to the scene.

7/28/2019—*Gilroy, California*
Nineteen-year-old Santino William Legan, armed with a semiautomatic rifle, kills three and wounds twelve, before he dies of a self-inflicted wound.

8/3/2019—*Walmart, El Paso, Texas*
Twenty-one-year-old Patrick Crusius is accused of using a semiautomatic rifle to kill twenty-two people and wound another twenty-five before police take him into custody. He is awaiting trial.

8/4/2019—*New Peppers Bar, Dayton, Ohio*
Twenty-four-year-old Connor Stephen Betts, armed with a modified semiautomatic weapon, kills nine people and injures twenty-seven before being killed by police.

8/31/2019—*Midland and Odessa, Texas*
Thirty-six-year-old Seth Aaron Ator, armed with a semiautomatic rifle, kills seven people and injures twenty-two during a shooting spree that ends when he is shot dead by police.

Final Thoughts
A Letter to Young People

I am writing this endnote just days after the mass shootings in El Paso, Texas, on August 3, and in Dayton, Ohio, on August 4, 2019. In the span of less than twenty-four hours, the lives of thirty-one ordinary, everyday people like you and me were abruptly ended, while dozens more were wounded. The dead included teenagers, parents, and grandparents. Their only mistake was being in the wrong place at the wrong time. They died without warning, never to see their loved ones again. The younger victims, people like yourselves, perished before they'd had much of a chance to live.

Here's a quote from a *Boston Globe* editorial inspired by those shootings: "America is sick. And it's getting sicker. Sick with hate, sick with rage. Sick with warped masculinity, sick with Internet-fueled radicalization and social isolation. Sick with racism, sick from social media that has breathed new life into old prejudices. And sick, of course, with guns."

It truly pains me to have to share that quote with you. It pains me to think that this is the condition of the country you are growing up in. Young people should not have to live in fear for their lives each time they leave their homes. They should not have to worry about the possibility of being slaughtered at school, or in a place of worship, or at the mall.

And yet, despite this terrible state of affairs, I see reason for hope. And that hope resides with you. For the first time since my own years as a teenager, when hundreds of thousands of us marched against the war in Vietnam, today the young people of this country are banding together in protest. At the forefront of this movement is the student-led March for Our Lives, organized in 2018 after the accused gunman Nikolas Cruz, armed with that legally purchased semiautomatic rifle, left a swath of death and injury through Marjory Stoneman Douglas High School in Parkland, Florida.

March for Our Lives (MFOL) has been instrumental in registering thousands of young voters, in the hope that these young people will push for greater gun control. MFOL also helped defeat numerous National Rifle Association–backed candidates during the 2018 midterm elections. In addition, they have organized marches and rallies, and have enlisted corporate sponsors in the fight for stronger gun laws. They have created a Peace Plan for a Safer America and are circulating petitions to support it. The plan demands that gun owners be licensed the same way motorists are; that semiautomatic assault weapons, which were banned by the US Congress from 1994 until 2004, be banned once again; and that a national buy-back program be instituted to reduce the number of privately owned firearms in this country.

The founders of March for Our Lives are the survivors

of the Parkland massacre, and in their communications to the public is the phrase "created by survivors, so you don't have to be one." It is early August 2019 as I write this, and thus far this year there have been twenty-two mass shooting incidents in the United States—roughly one every two weeks. One hundred twenty-five innocent, everyday people have been murdered, their lives cut short, their loved ones left bereft and devastated. And many more victims have been injured.

According to the *Washington Post*, there are nearly 400 million privately owned guns in our country of roughly 330 million people. No other country in the world comes close to having that many firearms per capita, nor does any other country suffer nearly the number of indiscriminate mass shootings that we have in the United States.

Only the willfully blind can fail to see the correlation.

The young people of this country were also dying unnecessarily in the 1960s. Back then it was due to an immoral war. In response, citizens banded together and fought back against a government that had become complicit with the military-industrial complex. People protested, marched, engaged in civil disobedience, and voted for candidates who opposed the war. Thanks to their efforts, the war ended and lives were spared. The same can happen today. By joining March for Our Lives and groups like it, young people can make their voices heard. By registering to vote, and helping others to register, young citizens can elect politicians who support gun control and can effect change in a government that has become a pawn of the National Rifle Association.

This year roughly 40,000 Americans will be killed by firearms in homicides, suicides, and accidents. Nearly 3,000 of them will be children and teens. An additional 15,600 children and teens will be injured in these incidents.

In 2016, Brandon Wolf was with his two best friends in the Pulse nightclub on the night forty-nine people were shot to death. He managed to survive, but both of his friends were killed. In 2018, following the Marjory Stoneman Douglas High School shooting, Brandon addressed this country and the politicians who run it: "After first graders were gunned down at Sandy Hook, what did you do? Not a damn thing. After forty-nine people, including my two brothers, were murdered at Pulse, what did you do? Not a damn thing. You plugged your ears and turned your eyes and hoped that we would stop talking. Now we're here again. Seventeen people are dead. Fourteen of them are children. And what did you do yesterday when given the chance to do something about it? Not a damn thing."

Brandon Wolf spoke the sorry truth: Politicians won't do a damn thing about mass shootings in this country . . . unless they are forced to. Unless their jobs are threatened. The more young people who register and vote for gun-control candidates, the more people protest and march and raise their voices against unsympathetic politicians, the more likely it is that a real change in gun laws can be accomplished. Until then, the only thing that will change is the rising numbers of the dead and injured in mass shootings. Just days after a gunman entered her school in

Parkland, Florida, and killed 17 people, Emma González, a senior at Marjory Stoneman Douglas High School, said this at a gun-control rally in Fort Lauderdale: "If you actively do nothing, people continually end up dead, so it's time to start doing something."

Amen.

If you would like to read and explore more about these issues, the following are some valuable resources:

vpc.org
The Violence Policy Center
Information on guns and youths
Works to stop gun death and injury, through research, education, advocacy, and collaboration.

pledge.org
Student Pledge Against Gun Violence
Organized to stop violence in schools. Honors the role that young people can play in reducing gun violence.

csgv.org
The Coalition to Stop Gun Violence
Seeks to prevent gun violence through data-driven policy development and aggressive advocacy.

everytown.org
Everytown for Gun Safety
Americans working together to end gun violence and build safer communities.

momsdemandaction.org
Moms Demand Action for Gun Sense in America
Demands that state and federal legislators enact legal
measures that will protect people from gun violence.

bradyunited.org
Brady United
Jim Brady, the White House press secretary, was
seriously wounded during an assassination attempt on
President Reagan. The organization named after Brady
endorses a comprehensive plan to make Americans safer
from gun violence.

giffords.org
Giffords
While serving as a US congresswoman, Gabby Giffords
was critically injured in a mass shooting. Her
organization is fighting for better gun control.

stophandgunviolence.org
Stop Handgun Violence
Committed to the prevention of gun violence, through
education, increased public awareness, effective law
enforcement, and common-sense gun laws.

keepgunsoffcampus.org
The Campaign to Keep Guns Off Campus
Believes that no one should have to live in constant fear
of their children dying or being seriously injured
in shootings.

neveragain.com/gun-control

NeverAgain

Dedicated to Elie Wiesel, Simon Wiesenthal, Martin Luther King Jr., and all those who have fought for human and civil rights and who fight against genocide.

Many of these sites can also provide printed pamphlets and other materials.

**Turn the page
for a sneak peek at
*Price of Duty.***

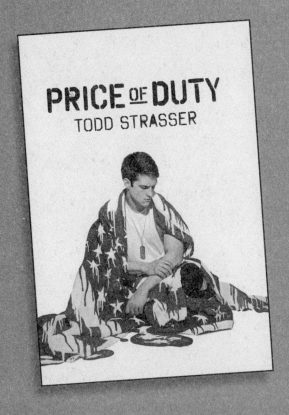

ALJAHIM

You are trained to be a soldier, not a hero. But sometimes the other thing happens.

BOOM! CRAUNK! Both sounds are unbelievably, painfully loud. Loud beyond imagining. Like your head being smashed between metal garbage can lids. So loud you can't believe you'll still have eardrums afterward. If you have time to believe anything. But you don't. There's no time.

A moment ago you were riding down a road in a Humvee. Now the vehicle's lying on its roof forty feet off the road and you're the only one left inside. Heavy munitions fire, screams, shouts, and explosions join the loud ringing in your ears. Metallic *plangs* ricocheting off the Humvee. Thudding *pocks* when rounds slam into the bulletproof windows. Inside the vehicle, you're hanging upside down, restrained by your seat harness. Half a dozen burning points of pain are distributed around your body.

Vision is a reddish blur. An IED headache has your brain in a death grip. Something warm is running up your cheek and into your right eye. It's bright red.

Someone nearby is screaming, *"I'm hit! I'm hit!"* Someone farther away is shouting, "Where's the triggerman? Find the triggerman!"

Bratta! Bratta! Bratta! Plang! Pock! Zang! Multiple weapons fire. It dawns on you that there is no one triggerman. There are dozens.

Boom! The Humvee is rocked by the blast of an RPG.

"Ahhh! Ahhhh!" More screams of pain.

Where are my buddies?

My eyepro's gone. There's nothing to protect my eyes from flying shrapnel and dirt. The reddish blur in my vision is blood. It's coming from a piece of shrapnel lodged painfully under my chin cup. How it got there, I'll never know. It's one of a dozen pieces of shrapnel that the Army docs will eventually remove from my body.

But right now most of those shrapnel are just vague burning points of pain. Right now it's all adrenaline, shock, shouts, and explosions. I'm upside down. Rollover training kicks in. Orient, establish three points of contact, brace, and release the seat harness. Egress. My gloved hand jerks the door handle, but the door won't open. Wait, my head is closer to the ground than my feet are. In this position, you don't push the door handle down. You pull it up.

An instant later I roll out into the heat, sunlight, and

mayhem. Intense machine gun and small arms fire bashing my eardrums. Supersonic lead bees whizzing past. But the firefight is good news. Someone on our side must be shooting back. The hot air stinks of gasoline and sulfur. A fusillade of bullets rips into the ground, spraying grains of dirt into my face and mixing with the blood in my eyes. I'm in the kill zone, in what must be far ambush conditions. How do I know it's not near ambush? Simple. If it was a near ambush, I'd be worm dirt by now.

More metallic bees whiz by. The closest ones cutting through the air inches from my head. I get prone, jam some QuikClot under my chin cup. Damn, that hurts, but it stops the bleeding. Blink the remaining blood out of my eyes and try to establish where the enemy fire is coming from. Glance around for cover. Where are my guys? Skitballs, Magnet, Clay? Remind myself that I'm in a mined area. I can't stay exposed like this for long without getting hit. But where will the land mines be if I move?

These thoughts race through my head in a matter of milliseconds.

"*Ahhhh! Ahhhh! I'm hit! Jake! I'm hit!*" It's Skitballs. He's somewhere to my right, where a lot of enemy fire is coming from.

I have to go get him.

JAKE

The prop plane touches down. I can see the crowd through the window. They're cheering, waving American flags—some small, some large. A handwritten bedsheet banner reads: WELCOME HOME, JAKE! OUR HERO!

A homemade cardboard sign taped to a broomstick: THANK YOU FOR SERVING OUR COUNTRY.

There must be two hundred people out there.

My heart beats harder. I've had weeks to prepare for this moment. Weeks to rehearse what to say and when to say it. Yes, I'm supposed to be a hero. I've been told that a thousand times since the ambush. Only I don't feel like a hero. When it's actually happening, you don't know you're being brave. You just do what you've been trained to do. What your instincts tell you to do.

You do it knowing there's a good chance you're going to die. You do it because you have to . . . if you hope to be able to live with yourself when it's over.

The plane that's brought me home to Franklin is provided by a company that collects donated miles and uses them to fly war heroes and wounded warriors around for "nonmilitary purposes." As we taxi toward the terminal, I start to recognize faces—Dad, Lori, Aurora, and the General are out in front. I've seen them dozens of times on Skype over the past six months, but now, seeing them this close makes my heart ache. I've missed them. It's going to be so good to be home.

The crowd can see me through the plane's window. They're waving, pumping their signs up and down, shouting words I can't hear through the glass. Meanwhile, my heart is drumming, my body taut at condition orange. My hands don't want to obey when I try to undo my seat belt. It's safe inside this plane. I'm protected . . . and alone.

Come on, Jake, I tell myself. *No one out there wants to hurt you.*

This should be easy, right? Just go out there and see your family, your friends, and a couple hundred adoring neighbors. Instead, it's as stressful as being in the lead Humvee of a convoy. As much as I've been looking forward to seeing everyone, I've been dreading this moment for weeks.

"Jake?" The pilot's come out of the cockpit and is leaning on the seat in front of me. He has a ruddy face and a mustache. Gray sideburns poke out from beneath his pilot's hat. With that frozen smile people wear when they're trying to mask concern, he nods at the window. "They're waiting for you."

"Yessir." I unbuckle the seat belt. Ironically, at moments like this, it's military training that gets me to do that which I wasn't sure I'd be able to do. My left leg juts out into the aisle because it's in a cast from the top of my thigh to my foot. I grab a crutch with one hand, and the top of the seat in front of me with the other.

"Need help?" the pilot offers.

"No, sir. Thank you, sir." I hoist myself up and position the crutches. Duck my head down the narrow aisle and turn out through the doorway. The crowd cheers, raises their banners, and waves flags. There's everything short of a brass band. The sun is bright and I'm glad I'm wearing shades. It feels hot for early June. With the scent of honeysuckle in the air come memories of carefree days lounging by swimming pools, flirting with pretty girls.

If only I didn't know now what I didn't know then.

I start down the airstairs. At Landstuhl, they taught me how to do stairs with crutches and not fall on my face. The plane's props have stopped turning and the cheering crowd surges forward. My body goes tense, on alert. You can tell yourself that these are family and friends, that this is secure and sheltered America, not a war-plagued foreign land filled with snipers and suicide bombers. But you can't simply turn off training and experience. My eyes dart automatically, searching for the telltale metallic glint of a weapon, the unnatural bulge of a suicide vest under a shirt.

Halfway down the steps, my heart is racing. My body

may have returned home, but my brain is still wired for war.

My family waits at the bottom of the airstairs. Lori and Aurora have tears in their eyes. They slide their arms inside the crutches, hug and kiss me. I'm enveloped in the different scents of their perfumes. My heart swells. It feels safe to be with them. They try not to stare at the jagged scar on my chin. They've seen it before on Skype, but here it is for real.

Dad pulls me close. "It's great to have you home." He seems to be blinking back tears.

The General gives me a bone-crushing handshake and claps a hand on my shoulder. "Congratulations, son. We're proud of you. You're a tremendous credit to our family."

Aurora keeps her arm around my waist and nestles close. The fragrance of her light brown hair delights my nostrils. I'm so glad to see her, so filled with gratitude that she waited for me. Plenty of guys had girlfriends who didn't. But she wrote letters and sent candy and thumb drives with movies on them. And she was almost always there when I wanted to Skype. What I've been through was bad, but it would have been so much worse without her.

This is the last stop on the "hero tour." My right wrist is sore from all the hands I've had to shake. I've learned to keep my left hand low at my side and in a loose fist. That way the damage is less noticeable. But my sister, Lori, knows what happened and reaches for it.

"Not here," I whisper.

The rest of the crowd presses in. My body stiffens. I've been on anti-anxiety meds for weeks. Otherwise, I might be doing a combat roll right now. But even with the pills, I'm still wound tight like a spring.

Up till now, I've always had a minder who's helped control the crowds. But not here. It's too loud, disorderly, and chaotic. Family friends want me to come to dinner. A TV crew wants me to give an interview. Strangers congratulate me on my bravery and thank me for my service. I can't keep track of who's touching, patting, grasping. There's no order, no space, no room to breathe.

Aurora slides between me and the crowd. She must feel the tension in my body, the tightness with which I clutch her waist. She tugs at Dad's sleeve, stretches up on her toes, and whispers in his ear.

Dad's forehead bunches, and he turns to the crowd. "Okay, everyone, thanks for being here. Jake's delighted that you've all come out to welcome him. But let's give him some room, okay? It's been a long trip and he's tired. He'll be home all week and I'm sure he'll make time to see all of you, but right now he needs to get—"

"Now, just a minute!" the General gruffly interrupts. "These people have given up part of their day to come out and stand here in the hot sun. The least they deserve is a few words from our conquering hero."

Damn!

* * *

What is a hero? I'd say that it's just about anyone who ever served in the military. Probably anyone who's ever gone to war. Definitely anyone who's spent more than a day at Forward Operating Base Choke Point, running for the bunkers every time the warning siren wailed and soldiers shouted, "Incoming!"

"*Ahhhhhhhhhhh!*" In the dusty dimness, my buddy Skitballs hugged his knees and let out a shriek that made us all jump. With the sirens blaring, we'd all just dived into this bunker. Skitballs—Jayden Skinner, dark-skinned, tall, lanky—was the last guy in. He'd barely gotten here when the first missile blast slammed the reinforced door shut behind him. Had he been a second slower, there'd probably only be bits and pieces of him now.

"Y'all okay, Skits?" Morpiss asked in the near dark.

The stream of curses Skitballs unleashed were strangely reassuring. It sounded more like the grunt we knew, the dude who signed up so he could pay off his girlfriend's credit card debt with the enlistment bonus. We waited while he calmed down, taking deep breaths, his fists clenching and unclenching. "Goddamn!" he groaned. "What kind of psycho bat whack is this? Incoming day and night. Can't sleep. Can't think straight. Am I the only one here going crazy?"

We all were. Skitballs was just the first to say it out loud.

"Go see the doc. He'll give you something," a voice came from the shadows deeper in the bunker. From an older, grizzled, sunbaked guy wearing corporal stripes.

Looked too old to be a noncommissioned officer. But they said life in a war zone aged you in dog years.

"Give me something?" Skitballs asked. "Like what?"

He'd soon find out. We all would.

Retired Major General Windborne (Windy) Granger is my grandfather, my mother's father, and a famous war hero. Around Franklin they call him the General, and he still expects everyone to follow his orders. For the most part, they do.

Standing in the hot sun on the airport tarmac, the crowd grows quiet. One of the stupidest things I ever read was about how some people fear public speaking more than death. Anyone who believes that hasn't come within a thousand yards of a lead slug traveling 1,700 miles per hour straight for your face. Give a soldier a choice between standing before a crowd of a hundred thousand and telling them about the five most embarrassing things that ever happened to him, or being in a Humvee rolling over an IED—improvised explosive device—loaded with eighty pounds of potassium chlorate? I guarantee you he'll gladly tell the whole crowd about that time his sister walked into the bathroom while he was busy getting to know Mary Five-Fingers.

With the General beside me, I give the crowd what he wants: "Thank you all for coming out to greet me. I feel honored that you took the time. I hope you've seen on TV or the internet, me saying how proud I am to be from

Franklin, where people have big hearts and strong values. It's really good to be home."

The crowd cheers until the General raises a hand and quiets them so he can also thank them for coming out (and remind them that he's the hero's grandfather). Then it's over. Dad takes my arm and guides me toward the General's big black Mercedes. Not many people around Franklin would be allowed to bring their cars onto the airport runway, but guess which famous retired general can?

Before we get to the car, Sam Washington plants himself in front of me. He's wearing his Junior Reserve Officers Training Corps instructor uniform with all the fruit salad. He's a Gulf War vet and was my JROTC instructor at Franklin High. Probably around fifty years old and still in top military shape. He pulls me into a bear hug, crutches and all. With his lips close to my ear, he whispers, "You okay, son?"

Here's how I *wish* I could answer: by telling him to go to hell.

Here's how I do answer: "Yessir."

Sam lets me out of the hug but holds me at arm's length. "So you'll come speak to the class tomorrow," he says loud enough for those around us to hear. "They all want to hear your story."

What story will I tell them?

He lets go, but there's someone behind him. She's wearing a baggy gray athletic T and cutoffs, and her brown hair is gathered up in a loose bun of dreadlocks spreading out like octopus tentacles. "Hi, I'm Brandi," she says with a bright smile. Her gray-green eyes are piercing. "I've been texting you? You haven't answered, probably because you get so many."

Near us, the General makes no attempt to hide his glower. Is he offended that she's dressed so informally (in his mind: disrespectfully) for this event? Or is the explanation both simpler and uglier: that she's not the "correct" color?

"I'm from the *Franklin Frontier*," Brandi goes on, undeterred. "I know you've already given, like, a thousand interviews, but it would be so great if you'd give one to your former high school."

"I'm sorry, miss," the General harrumphs. "Jake's just come an awful long way. Now isn't the—"

"Oh, I didn't mean now." When Brandi cuts him short, my grandfather's eyes narrow and his jaw goes tight. Interrupting is something you just don't do to the General. The funny thing is, I get the feeling she knows this. Or at least senses it. And she cut in anyway.

"Maybe tomorrow?" Brandi says. "At school? After the JROTC class?"

"Sure," I tell her, pretending not to notice my grandfather's frown.

The General's driver holds the Mercedes's door open. A driver and car is one of the retirement perks some generals get. Now that I've gotten this close to Aurora, I hate to leave her again. But she understands. I give her a kiss and tell her I'll see her later. Inside the car, I have to ride in front because that's the only seat with enough legroom for my cast. Lori, Dad, and the General sit in the back.

When the Mercedes starts to move, my hands automatically slide toward my chest before I catch myself and place them in my lap. It's just muscle memory. The first time I rode in a Humvee with Brad, he told me to keep my hands inside my armor. I slid them through the arm holes, where they naturally landed on my pecs. I sat that way for a while, but my hands began to get hot and it felt weird to have them over my pecs anyway. So I took them out. Brad's eyes slid in my direction. I could see he disapproved.

About a month later a suicide bomber in an old car loaded with explosives rammed a Humvee just outside the wire and blew the guys inside to smithereens. Romeo Squad was on security detail that day, and Brad lined us up for casualty collection. His eyes went right past me, then stopped and returned as if he'd remembered something. "And especially you, Liddell. Go out and find the pieces. All of them."

He wasn't talking about pieces of the Humvee.

It was probably one of the worst things I ever had to do. One of the many chores you won't see in any Army recruiting commercial. Morpiss and I puked. A couple of other guys couldn't even do it. And, of course, as if Brad had known, there was a hand.

Now, in the privacy of the Mercedes, Lori wants to see *my* hand, which, luckily, is still attached to my body.

I drape my left arm over the seat. My hand is missing the pinkie and the distal phalanx of the ring finger. I hear a loud sniff. Lori starts to cry. I look back and my eyes meet Dad's. I wonder if he's thinking what I'm thinking. Losing a finger is nothing compared to what others have lost. I'd give my whole left arm if it meant Morpiss could get back half of what he's lost.

And Skitballs.

And Clay.

For what?

"You okay?" Dad asks.

"Of course he's okay," the General says. "He's a god-damn war hero."

THE GENERAL

The General was a corporal in Vietnam. His squad was ambushed in the jungle and the squad leader killed. My grandfather took command, broke the team in two, and ordered a fire-and-maneuver retreat to a point where they hoped to link up with reinforcements. The skirmish was fierce and, at times, hand-to-hand. Despite being wounded in the shoulder and arm, my grandfather never quit. After the squad linked up with the reinforcements and turned the retreat into an assault, he kept fighting and refused medical treatment until it was over.

They awarded him the Bronze Star. I wonder if he felt as weird about what happened then as I feel now. No, not a chance. He's always been gung-ho.

Guess I was like that once.

Not anymore.

The Army brass is still in the process of deciding what level of valor medal I'll be awarded. I've heard that they're considering me for the Silver Star. One step up from the bronze, one level higher than the General's.

Would I dare refuse it?

On the way home from the airport the signs in front of the fast-food places, the car wash, and the elementary school all say, WELCOME HOME, JAKE LIDDELL, OUR HERO.

At our house a silver-gray Jeep Wrangler in the driveway sparkles in the sunlight. I haven't heard anything about Dad or Lori getting a new car. The garage doors are open and inside are Dad's Cherokee and Lori's Honda.

The Mercedes stops behind the Wrangler. The Jeep's tail reflectors have that new-car shimmer.

No one gets out. I feel the General's hand clap my shoulder from behind. "You've earned it, son."

Is he serious?

We pile out. The Jeep's got that straight-from-the-showroom smell. I'm overwhelmed. From the time Lori and I were little, Dad made it clear that we weren't one of those families where the kids got everything they wanted. Some kids in our neighborhood were given cars as soon as they were old enough to drive. We were given advice on how to find a good used vehicle that we could afford with our savings.

"You don't have to do this, sir," I tell the General. I'd hug him, but he hates being hugged almost as much as he hates being called "Grandpa." So instead I endure another one of his bone-crushing handshakes.

"You deserve it," he says. "You're a real military man now."

It's no accident that he says this in front of my father, who, through no fault of his own, has spent his military career as a PowerPoint Ranger. Dad's a lieutenant colonel at the base here in Franklin, and the General never misses an opportunity to remind him that all he's ever been is a desk jockey. He's never gone to war; never tasted battle the way "real" soldiers do.

The General checks his watch. "I'll let you get some R and R." He heads back to the Mercedes, where his driver is holding the door. And then he's gone.

Dad, Lori, and I stay in the driveway with the new Jeep. It's completely unnecessary . . . and if I work up the guts to do what I believe I should do, I won't be the only one who feels that way. *Sure hope the General kept the receipt.*

I glance at Lori. She's two years older than me, so we've always had a brother/sister competition over who got what. But when my eyes meet hers, there's not a trace of resentment.

"You do deserve it," she says.

For a moment, I can't hold her gaze, and have to look away. When our eyes meet again, she's frowning as if she can sense that something's wrong.

"All right." Dad claps his hands. "Let's get you inside and settled."